"I'll want to be the center of the lady's life."

As he spoke, Tessa searched Patrick's face for a glint of humor, but his eyes and mouth were deadly serious. Disappointment that he was so narrow-minded engulfed her.

"Wipe that accusation off your face," he stated. "I'm only telling you what most men want. Unfortunately they haven't the guts to say it, or the strength of mind to stick to it. They fall in love and their intelligence goes haywire! Not that I'd want a complete homebody. Merely a woman who'll love me enough to make my life hers."

"You must introduce me to this paragon when you find her," Tessa said.

"Oh, I haven't started searching yet. I enjoy my freedom too much to think of curtailing it."

ROBERTA LEIGH wrote her first book at the age of nineteen and since then has written more than seventy romance novels, as well as many books and film series for children. She has also been an editor of a woman's magazine and produced a teen magazine, but writing romance fiction remains one of her greatest joys. She lives in Hampstead, London, and has one son.

Books by Roberta Leigh

HARLEQUIN PRESENTS
1026—A RACY AFFAIR
1043—TOO BAD TO BE TRUE
1066—AN IMPOSSIBLE MAN TO LOVE
1092—NO MAN'S MISTRESS
1115—STORM CLOUD MARRIAGE
1217—NOT WITHOUT LOVE
1275—MAN ON THE MAKE
1298—A MOST UNSUITABLE WIFE

HARLEQUIN ROMANCE
1196—DARK INHERITANCE
1269—PRETENCE
1424—THE VENGEFUL HEART
1696—MY HEART'S A DANCER
1715—IN NAME ONLY
1783—CINDERELLA IN MINK
1800—SHADE OF THE PALMS
1893—IF DREAMS CAME TRUE

ROBERTA LEIGH

it all depends on love

Harlequin Books

TORONTO • NEW YORK • LONDON
AMSTERDAM • PARIS • SYDNEY • HAMBURG
STOCKHOLM • ATHENS • TOKYO • MILAN

Harlequin Presents first edition May 1991
ISBN 0-373-11363-3

Original hardcover edition published in 1990
by Mills & Boon Limited

IT ALL DEPENDS ON LOVE

CHAPTER ONE

'GO AWAY and rest for three months and don't dare come back earlier,' Sir Denis Denzil told Tessa Redfern, and, though she wanted to plead that a month would be enough, she remained silent. No one argued with the great surgeon, least of all herself, who had been his assistant since qualifying as a doctor five years ago.

And what a tough five years they had been! She had worked herself into the ground—literally, it now seemed, for last week she had collapsed in the operating theatre, though a battery of tests had shown nothing more sinister than total fatigue.

'Buy yourself some pretty clothes and go on a cruise,' Sir Denis broke into her thoughts. 'Or hibernate in the country and pick flowers. But, whatever you do, don't pick up a knife!'

Easy advice to give, but not to follow, Tessa thought gloomily, when your lifelong ambition since you were ten had been to be a surgeon!

'I'll stay at my godfather's house,' she said. 'Unfortunately he's in New Zealand at the moment, studying the bird life, but his housekeeper will enjoy herself mothering me.'

Sir Denis studied his registrar's fragile features: wide amber eyes fringed by thick, dark lashes in a beguiling elfin face, milk and roses complexion—more milk than roses at the moment—a delicately shaped mouth, a firm chin, and soft curling red-gold hair.

For all she was only twenty-seven—and looked nineteen—she was the most brilliant assistant he had had,

5

and a great future lay ahead of her. His mouth twitched humorously as he remembered their first meeting, and her efforts to make herself appear older: hair scraped into a bun, horn-rimmed glasses she didn't need, and voluminous clothes to add bulk to her figure. Thank goodness that phase had only lasted till she'd become sufficiently confident not to hide the fact that she was a pocket-sized Venus who could never aspire to be the Amazon of her dreams!

'No boyfriends, Tessa?'

'No one serious,' she said, fleetingly remembering Christopher.

'Not for want of their trying, I'm sure,' came the paternalistic response.

'I'm not interested in romantic involvements,' she said firmly. 'Time enough when I've made it to the top.'

'That's foolish thinking, if you don't mind my saying so. Our work requires enormous concentration and physical stamina, as you well know, and if our personal lives are happy, our professional ones are the better for it.' He pushed aside the notes in front of him and leaned forward, a spare, angular figure. 'Not everyone wants marriage and a family, I grant you that, but I'd be surprised if *you* didn't.'

'Of course I do,' she admitted. 'But in the future, not now. Being your assistant doesn't leave time for a personal life, Sir Denis! I'm not complaining,' she added hurriedly, 'simply stating a fact.'

'Which my wife will endorse!' he smiled. 'But if your husband were a doctor, perhaps, who'd understand... And you *do* get maternity leave!'

Tessa laughed. 'Hey, you're jumping the gun!'

Noon the next day found her driving along a leafy Oxfordshire lane to Greentrees—her godfather's small Queen Anne house which had been her home since she was four. As the imposing entrance gates to Finworth

Hall flashed by, she was surprised to note they had been newly painted. So crotchety old Lord Finworth had finally spent something on the place! She was curious to know if he'd renovated the house too, but it was too far down the drive to see. Still, Mrs Benson was sure to know what was going on. Uncle Martin jokingly called her the eyes and ears of the world!

Greentrees came in sight, elegant and compact in its old-world garden, and as she drew to a stop by the front door she experienced a contented sense of homecoming. If only Uncle Martin were here! He and his wife had been close friends of her parents, and after their death on a mountaineering expedition Uncle Martin and his wife had given her a home and treated her as the child they'd never had. Aunt Ellen had died when Tessa was twelve, since when Mrs Benson had dispensed motherly comfort alongside her delicious cooking.

Tessa was searching for her key when the front door was opened by a plump woman in her fifties.

'Tessa! How lovely to——' Mrs Benson broke off as she was knocked aside by a huge, shaggy bundle of brown and white fur, three quarters sheepdog, one quarter heaven knew what, and wholly lovable, who greeted Tessa with rapturous barks and flailing tail before dashing round the back of the house and out of sight.

'Drat that dog!' the woman exclaimed. 'There's a gap in the garden wall and he keeps going through it to the Hall.'

'Lord Finworth will skin him,' Tessa said, remembering the irascible man's dislike of animals.

'Not any more, my dear. He died five months ago. Didn't Mr Anderson mention it when you saw him in London?'

'So he did. I'd quite forgotten. Age must be catching up on me!'

'Pressure of work, more like it,' Mrs Benson grunted, giving her the once-over. 'You're thin as a pin. Thank goodness you're being sensible and taking a holiday.'

Returning the woman's motherly hug, Tessa heaved her case from the car and entered the house. The familiar smell of lavender polish and home-baked bread assailed her, and, leaving her things in the hall, she followed Mrs Benson into the kitchen for a longed-for cup of tea.

As she drank the delicious Darjeeling, and ate one of Mrs Benson's incomparable scones, thick with cream and jam, she admitted that Sir Denis was right, as always. She was tight as a drum and sorely in need of a rest.

Scratching on the back door heralded the return of Henry, who bounded over to her and placed two large paws on her shoulders.

'*I* never get that,' Mrs Benson grumbled.

'Not even for a marrowbone?' Tessa ducked her head to avoid Henry's wet tongue.

'The ones I give him can't compare with those he gets at the Hall. Mr and Mrs Withers spoil him rotten.'

'Are they the new owners?'

'Goodness, no. They're Mr Harper's cook and butler.'

'What are the Harpers like?'

'It's Harper in the singular,' Mrs Benson stated. 'He's Lord Finworth's nephew, and he inherited the place. A proper tycoon, he is. Off in his helicopter at the drop of a hat.'

'And I came here for peace and quiet!'

'It mostly *is* quiet,' the housekeeper assured her. 'They're a very well-behaved lot and keep themselves to themselves.'

'Lot?' Tessa's curiosity stirred further. 'I thought there was only Mr Harper?'

'And his think-tank.'

'His what?'

'Think-tank. He owns Harper Software, and has about a dozen people here, dreaming up programs for him.'

Tessa's knife, raised to butter her second scone, stopped in mid-air. Harper Software was famous throughout the world for its brilliant software for industry and medicine.

'I'm surprised he's allowed to use the Hall for business,' she commented.

'He only has this group here—his factory's in Kent.'

'One big happy family, then.'

'They are,' Mrs Benson correctly read Tessa's expression. 'Too busy for fun and games.'

'Not surprising, with the big boss keeping an eye on them!'

'He doesn't. According to Mrs Withers, he spends most of his time in the west wing—he's turned it into his private home. You won't recognise the house and garden, love. It's a fair treat.'

Tessa agreed whole-heartedly when, shortly afterwards, she gazed through her bedroom window past their own compact garden to the sweeping acres of well-tended lawns and carefully trimmed shrubs and trees. Although the imposing frontage of the Hall was hidden by trees, the section she glimpsed showed new paint, careful repointing of brickwork, and gleaming windows.

The soft purr of an arriving car—no helicopter, thankfully—made her curious as to why Mr Harper had chosen to site his boffins in rural splendour rather than with his factory in Kent. Still, many large companies were moving to the country, and as he'd inherited the Hall and was a bachelor like his uncle he had obviously decided to put the house to use.

Recollecting Sir Denis's order that she start thinking of a personal life, she debated whether to invite the 'think-tank' over for an informal 'getting to know the neighbours' party. Of course, she'd check with Mr

Harper first. If he was a curmudgeon like his uncle, he might not want his employees to fraternise with the locals in case it deflected them from their work.

Turning from the window, she unpacked, washed, and went to put in a call to her godfather. He was delighted to hear she was taking a three-month sabbatical, and asked if she would care to join him.

'Some rest I'd have,' she teased. 'You'd have me up all hours watching your beloved birds! No, thanks, Nunc,' she used her favourite word for him, 'I'm happy to remain here.'

'Then you'll be able to take care of Henry while Mrs Benson's on holiday. But see you don't spoil him.'

'I won't,' she promised, though she knew Henry would make it hard for her not to.

Returning to her room for a book, she glanced through the window and saw him wriggle his large body through a gap in the stone wall, then gambol over the grass to the back door. How infuriating it must be for the people at the Hall to have an oversized hound drooling over them when they were trying to work! First thing to-morrow she'd see about mending the gap. Come to think of it, she was too tired even to read. Stepping out of her dress, she relaxed under the duvet, unable to believe she wasn't on call at the hospital, one ear alert to her bleeper. What bliss having nothing to do except please herself...

Dusk was casting its purple net over the landscape when a gentle touch on her shoulder brought her instantly to her feet, ready to run to a patient.

'Sorry to wake you,' Mrs Benson apologised, 'but I didn't want you sleeping through the night and missing dinner. Shall I bring it up to you on a tray?'

'Thanks a million for the offer,' Tessa yawned, 'but no. I know I've worked myself into the ground, but I'm not an invalid. What time is it, anyway?'

'Nearly nine.'

'Heavens! You should have woken me earlier.'

'Why? You came here to rest, didn't you?'

'There's a difference between resting and being slothful! Give me ten minutes and I'll be down.'

Padding into the bathroom, Tessa undressed and stepped under the shower, enjoying the force of the jets plastering her red-gold curls to her head, and forming rivulets upon her small, tip-tilted breasts, flat stomach and shapely legs.

She found it strange to be suddenly conscious of her body. It was as if she had been so busy cutting into other people's these past few years that she hadn't realised she had one of her own! All she'd had time for was throwing on her clothes, bolting down her meals, and rushing between home and hospital.

Stepping from the shower, she rubbed the steam from the mirrored wall and stared at her face as if for the first time too. What a wreck! Her amber eyes were shadowed with fatigue, and were enormous in her hollow-cheeked face. She blinked the water from her lashes, wishing they were longer, and knowing she should be content that they were several shades darker than her hair and thick as a brush. But she wasn't displeased with her nose, which was small and faintly *retroussé*, and she quite liked her mouth, with its full upper lip. If she were six inches taller she'd be worth a whistle! She smiled as she recalled the times Uncle Martin had reminded her that good things often came in small packages!

Donning a housecoat, she went down to dinner and, an hour later, replete with shepherd's pie and a Charentais melon, Tessa sank into a puffy brown velvet armchair in the living-room.

She glanced affectionately at Henry, sprawled on a rug in front of the unlit fire. With his black nose hidden between his paws, and his back legs splayed straight out behind him, it was a challenge to guess which was the back and front of him! How lucky I was to grow up here, she mused, eyes ranging over the much-loved paintings, books and Chinese jade figures that filled the shelves. Not only had she had the love of an erudite, kindly man, but she had also been encouraged to share his many interests.

A marvellous man, she mused lovingly. If she could find a thirty-years-younger version of him, she'd have no problem taking Sir Denis's advice to marry. But this was highly unlikely, for Uncle Martin was a one-off, and she would do better to concentrate on her career and forget about marriage.

CHAPTER TWO

THAT night Tessa dreamed she was with her godfather at Mount Bruce Bird Sanctuary in New Zealand, lying in a hide-out by a lake, waiting for dawn and the birds to awaken.

And it was bird-song which brought her back to consciousness, though Henry's barking reminded her where she was. She stretched and yawned, luxuriating in the knowledge that she had nothing to do all day except do nothing!

The delicious aroma of frying bacon provided her with the impetus to get dressed, and, curls abounce from the vigorous brush strokes she hadn't treated them to in months, she ran downstairs—a child of a woman in faded jeans and sweater.

'Nothing like a good night's rest to bring the roses into your cheeks,' Mrs Benson remarked, setting a plate of steaming oatmeal before her.

'Plus spoiling and good food,' Tessa smiled, tucking into the porridge.

'It's such a beautiful day,' the housekeeper went on. 'I've put the cushions on the hammock for you.'

'First, I'm going to see about that gap in the wall.'

Breakfast over, she collected the local paper from the front doorstep, tucked it under her arm to read later, and set off down the garden to examine Henry's escape route.

How could anyone choose to live in a city? she wondered, absorbing the glorious stillness around her and drawing in deep breaths of flower-scented air. London

rarely had skies as blue as this. Her eyes ranged the im-
maculately kept lawns, ablaze with flowers and shrubs,
to the grey stone wall that divided Greentrees from the
Hall. What on earth had dislodged the centuries-old
stones?

Close up she was none the wiser, and, hoping the other
side might offer an explanation, she bent and crawled
through the breach.

Immediately she had her answer. A tall cypress some
yards away had spread its roots under the foundation
and weakened it. Her eyes glinted. Putting it to rights
was Mr Harper's responsibility—unless he didn't object
to Henry pestering him!

'Practising to be an ostrich?' a terse male voice questioned behind her.

Startled, Tessa remained motionless. Ostrich? Then,
realising that bending had put her in a less than dig-
nified position, she hurriedly straightened and turned,
raising her eyes to introduce herself to the man. And
how far she had to raise them! He was well over six feet,
and the handsomest male she had ever met. She took in
the glossy chestnut hair atop a narrow, fine-boned face,
eyes the blue of sapphires, marked by thick, winging
eyebrows, a strong nose and a wide, curling mouth: top
lip well defined, lower one full and sensual.

Tessa had seen many handsome men in her time—as
a surgeon she had frequently had the opportunity of appraising them at leisure!—but never had she encountered one whose impact on her was so specific and
profound. Not only did he make her aware of every part
of his body—slim, yet wide-shouldered, with well-
muscled arms tapering to beautifully shaped hands, and
firm thighs descending to strong, sinewy legs—but also
intensely aware of her own.

Though his survey of her was general, she was conscious of her breasts tingling as though he had stroked

them, and her stomach tightening with a desire that spread lower and grew stronger as it did. This was insane! But, insane or not, warmth permeated every cell and fibre of her being, and she experienced a sense of excitement totally new to her.

Snap out of it, she ordered herself. You're simply tired and a prey to your imagination. If you'd met him three months ago, you wouldn't have given him a second glance. Yet as she tried to reassure herself she knew he'd have had the same impact on her whenever they had met. Call it fate, luck or chemistry, the end result amounted to the same: for the first time in her life she was physically overwhelmed by a man.

'Finished?' he asked, frowning at her with those incredibly blue eyes of his.

'Finished?'

'Looking me over. If there's any looking to be done, *I'm* the one to be doing it.'

'Oh, really?'

'It's quite usual,' he stated. 'I've no intention of buying a pig in a poke.'

She blinked. Was he mad? She'd play along with him anyway. 'I'm not *selling* a pig in a poke.'

'But you're selling *yourself*, aren't you? And I've had so many loonies applying, I intend making sure I pick the right one.'

'Applying for what?' Tessa questioned.

A well-shod foot nudged the newspaper she had dropped to the ground when examining the wall. 'The advertisement, of course. I assume you're here in answer to it?'

'Advertisement?'

'Dammit! Are you a parrot as well as an ostrich?'

'There's no need to be rude,' Tessa said spiritedly, and was about to walk away when the truth of the situation dawned on her. This man had put an advert in the local paper, and had mistaken her for an applicant! Though why she should then start examining a garden wall . . . Still, he had said a few loonies had applied, and he obviously thought her another!

'I'm afraid you're mistaken, Mr—er——'

'Patrick Harper.'

Hell's bells! *He* was the tycoon who'd inherited the Hall. She had imagined him older and shorter, with greying hair and conservative clothes, instead of which he was in his early thirties, tall and rangy, and clad in navy trousers and blue silk sweater.

'Well?' he asked briskly. 'Aren't you going to tell me about yourself? Or do you expect me to engage you on looks alone?'

He had touched a vulnerable spot and her hackles rose. All through medical school she had had to be twice as good as anyone else to prove that brainpower, intelligence and aptitude had nothing to do with one's appearance.

'Physical attributes neither detract from nor enhance one's ability, Mr Harper.'

'I wouldn't say that,' he drawled. 'Looks are highly relevant for a strip-tease artist.'

'But you're not advertising for one,' she countered, fast losing the impetus to tell him who she was.

'Damned right I'm not.' He raked her with a sharp blue glance. 'Not that you meet my requirements, anyway. You're only a kid.'

The impulse to hit him was almost irresistible. 'I'm older than I look,' was all she said.

'Which is?'

'Guess.'

'Eighteen.'

'Spot on!' Unexpectedly, Tessa's good humour reasserted itself and she decided to play along with him a while longer. How abject he'd be when she finally put him wise! Well, perhaps not 'abject'. She couldn't imagine his ever being *that*!

'I suppose I may as well interview you now you're here,' he muttered. 'You can't be worse than the others.'

He swung away from her, long legs carrying him ten yards across the grass before she managed to catch up with him. Running to keep pace with his stride, she was panting by the time he stopped beneath the shade of a beech tree and parked himself on the bench ringing it, a narrow hand indicating her to do the same.

Meekly she complied, and waited for him to speak. He waited too, and, curbing her amusement, she asked sweetly, 'What does the job entail?'

'Exactly what it said in the advert.'

This stumped her. 'One can't put everything in an advertisement,' she rejoined finally.

'Basically, I need someone to stand in for one or other of my domestic staff on their days off, or if one of them is ill. I can't afford any disruption in my household,' he explained. 'It has to run like a computer.'

'Computers can go wrong,' she said, straight-faced.

'Mine don't.'

His tone brooked no argument. Not that she would have given him one, for Harper machines and software were renowned for their reliability.

'Well?' he went on, looking down his perfect nose at her. 'Think you can manage the job, Miss—er——?'

'Tessa Redfern.'

'You live locally?'

'Yes.' At least that was no lie. Aware of his eyeing her old jeans and sweater with distaste, she said hastily, 'I don't usually dress this way.'

'I should hope not.'

Tessa wanted to kick herself for giving him the chance to insult her. How she dressed was no concern of his, and if he didn't stop staring at her so disapprovingly she'd walk off. No, she wouldn't, for she couldn't remember when she had last enjoyed herself so much!

'I doubt it will work,' he muttered, running slim fingers through unruly chestnut hair. 'You're far too young. What have you done since leaving school?'

The question caught her unawares and she stared at him dumbly.

'Don't tell me you're a drop-out, living on social security and thinking the world owes you a living?' he exclaimed.

'I've answered *this* job advert, haven't I?' Tessa's wits had returned and she gave him a haughty glare.

'Hmm,' he muttered, before lithely rising and taking a notebook from his pocket. 'What's your address and telephone number, in case I decide to engage you?'

The patronising... As if she'd tell him! Except she didn't have much choice, for he would notice her going back to Greentrees! Taking the bull by the horns, she said brightly, 'I live next door.'

A chestnut eyebrow winged up. 'How come?'

'I—er—I'm house-sitting for Mr Anderson.'

'You mean he's given the run of his home to a girl like you?'

'That's enough!' Tessa jumped to her feet. 'What do you mean "a girl like you"? You know nothing about me!'

'Except that you're a half-pint female with a gallon of a temper and an ounce of brain!'

'Then why bother interviewing me?'

'Because I'm amused you think yourself capable of doing the job.'

'It sounds dead easy to me. You don't need a great brain to stand in for a maid or a cook on her day off.'

'So I take it you're cordon bleu?' he questioned coolly.

'Er—not exactly, but—but I'm a dab hand at meat and two veg, and I've a light one with pastry.'

'You're quitting your job next door, then?'

Only for a second was Tessa at a loss. Then she shook her head so vigorously that her red-gold curls bounced— the sort of gesture an eighteen-year-old might make. 'I've hardly anything to do there. Mr Anderson's housekeeper is teaching me the ropes before she goes on holiday. But there's little to learn, and I'm free most of the time.'

'And when she's away?'

'I can manage the two jobs. All I have to do is dust and take care of the dog.'

'I assume you have references?'

'How can I, when I'm a drop-out?'

Patrick Harper's beautifully cut mouth pursed, leaving Tessa so enthralled by its shape that she didn't hear his reply.

'What did you say?' she asked brightly.

'I said,' he repeated slowly, 'that I'm amazed Mr Anderson engaged you.'

'Is that so?' She made herself glare at him. 'For your information, he considers himself a good judge of character—which *you* obviously aren't!'

Patrick Harper's lower lip tightened with restrained temper. 'Have you ever trained for anything?'

'Not likely! Life's too short to waste it in some boring nine-to-five job.'

The chestnut head tilted incredulously, and a shaft of sunlight gave the hair reddish glints. 'Doing something worthwhile with your life need not necessitate boring work. You could be a gardener, a nursery school teacher, a nurse.'

'A nurse?' Tessa raised her voice an octave at the suggestion. 'I can't think of anything worse! That blood and pain and—ugh!'

'All right, you've made your point,' he said frigidly. 'If you're happy to waste your life, so be it.'

'I'm hardly wasting it.' She widened her eyes at him. 'I'm only eighteen, and most of it's in front of me.'

His mouth quirked with the first sign of humour. 'Don't bat those thick lashes at me, Miss Redfern, I'm practically old enough to be your father.'

'You'd have had to start young!'

'Let's say I'm sufficiently older than you to regard you as a child. Though in five years' time I mightn't be averse to being batted at by those cat's eyes of yours!'

'You'll be too old for me then,' she said cheekily, and sauntered away from him in the direction of Greentrees.

'Hang on a minute,' he called. 'Don't you want the job?'

'You mean you'd take me on?'

'I may not have a choice. I'll wait a few days and see if I get anyone better.'

'Good luck, then, Mr Harper.' Reaching the damaged secton of wall, she stopped. 'It's the roots of *your* cypress that have dislodged the stones,' she called to him. 'You'd better have it fixed.'

'I'll tell my estate manager to look into it.'

Only when she was out of his sight and hearing did she let her amusement ripple into laughter. It had been naughty of her to carry on the joke so long, but Mr High and Mighty needed pulling down a peg or two, and she had been unable to resist the challenge.

The word 'challenge' stopped her in her tracks. She'd be in a cleft stick if no suitable person applied to him and he decided to engage her! The idea was so outlandish that she dismissed it. If he required someone capable of standing in for his housekeeper as well as other staff, he'd be crazy to take on the flighty girl she had made herself out to be.

And Patrick Harper was anything but crazy!

CHAPTER THREE

FOUR days of doing nothing except eat, sleep and laze found Tessa ready to bite the dog.

Dropping the book she was reading, she considered ways of making the days go faster, but could think of nothing bar the supercilious face of Patrick Harper. If she were given one wish it would be to see his discomfiture when he learned her identity and how easily she had duped him.

And that might be pretty soon, once the local grapevine discovered she was staying at Greentrees!

However, if she steered clear of the village, and persuaded Mrs Benson to keep quiet . . . Her lips curved upwards at the prospect of making a fool of her smart-alec neighbour. It would teach him not to judge anyone on appearance alone. Of course, he'd first have to offer her the job.

But what fun if he did! It was the perfect answer to her boredom. Mischievously she began thinking of jokes to play on him. After all, an eighteen-year-old drop-out would be like a hair shirt to a dynamic tycoon who was only happy on the go!

Brushing an insect from her face, she let her thoughts drift to soft-spoken Christopher, whom she had nearly married four years ago. Odd to be thinking of him when she hadn't done so for ages—until Sir Denis had mentioned boyfriends, that was. How would her life have turned out if she had listened to her heart instead of her head, and given up a promising career to share the rigours of the Third World with him?

Yet Jane had loved him enough to do it without question, abandoning her profession as a lawyer to live with him in a remote village in India. But Christopher was in the past, and she knew his way of life would never have made her happy.

Wryly she recollected his hurt at her refusal to marry him. For all his gentleness, he'd displayed his own brand of chauvinism, failing to see that she had as much right to follow *her* career as he to follow *his*. She'd bet a penny to a pound Patrick Harper thought in the same way, for everything he'd said indicated arrogance. No need to ask if he saw women as second-class citizens—third class, more likely! Which should make fooling him all the sweeter.

Chuckling, she swung herself off the hammock and went to take a cool shower before supper.

Her reflection in the bathroom mirror pleased her. She was definitely less haggard, and her skin was tinged with pink. The dark rings under her eyes weren't quite as pronounced, and returning vitality made her hair more gold than red! Another month, and even Sir Denis would approve of the change in her!

Thinking of him reminded her of his comments about her lack of a personal life. He was right. Although she felt and appeared younger than her years, the calendar showed she was twenty-seven—time to admit there was more to life than an operating theatre!

It was time to resume a social life, contact old friends, join a drama circle or operatic society. She enjoyed singing and acting. She grinned hugely. With luck, she might get a chance to act opposite her next-door neighbour!

She was still amused by the idea when she went into the kitchen.

'I'm glad to see you bright and happy,' Mrs Benson approved, starting to carve the roast.

'I was thinking of Mr Harper.'

'I'm sure many young ladies do! I've only seen him once—the day he came storming in here with Henry—and he was handsome as a film star.'

'There's more to a man than a pretty face!' Tessa commented, unfolding her napkin.

'I'll grant you that, but Mrs Withers says he's also a real gentleman.'

'Has she worked for him long?'

'She and her husband have been with the family since Mr Harper was a boy. Seems the girls were chasing him when he was in short trousers!'

'And no one has yet caught him?'

'No, nor likely to,' Mrs Benson sniffed. 'Seems he gets what he wants without marriage. Girls these days are fools!'

Eager to learn more about her neighbour, Tessa tried to keep the conversation flowing. 'What's he like with people other than girlfriends?'

'According to Mrs Withers his employees stay forever.'

'Maybe he pays extra well!'

'It's more than that. She says he treats everyone as his equal.'

Not always, Tessa thought amusedly, pricking up her ears as the housekeeper added, 'I believe he has a very high-powered assistant. She's——' the woman's eyes shot to the clock on the mantelshelf, and she pushed back her chair '—gracious, if I don't hurry I'll be late for my church meeting!'

Frustrated, Tessa watched her bustle into the hall. Drat that meeting! Just when she was getting to the interesting part!

'I've fed Henry,' Mrs Benson called, 'so don't go giving him titbits. And don't clear away either. Go into the sitting-room and watch telly!'

Ignoring the injunction, Tessa loaded the dishwasher and tidied up before settling on to the sofa with a murder book. Two hours later, eyes glued to the penultimate page, she only vaguely registered the series of happy barks coming from the fireside.

'Be quiet, Henry!' she ordered, and, when he refused, tore her eyes from the page and saw he was wagging his tail at something behind her.

Glancing round, she spied Patrick Harper peering through the french windows. Hiding her elation, she remained where she was, and he rapped imperiously on the glass. Slowly she swung herself off the sofa to let him in.

Henry's ecstatic barking blotted out conversation, and she tried to shush him.

'You won't do any good that way,' the man called above the noise, and, catching Henry's collar with one hand, he forced the dog's rump to the ground with the other. 'Some dogs don't bark in the sitting position,' he grunted. Remember that.'

'Yes, Mr Harper,' she said meekly. 'You certainly have a knack with them.'

'It's simply a matter of showing them you're the master. Same as with women.'

Swallowing hard, Tessa ignored the remark, noting with disgust that Henry was positively drooling at Patrick Harper's feet.

'Damn fool dotes on me,' he muttered, going to an armchair with Henry at his heels.

'He obviously responds to a firm hand.' It was an effort for Tessa to keep the sarcasm from her voice. 'And I can see you're very fond of dogs.'

'In their place.'

'Which is?'

'As guard dogs, hunting dogs, dogs for the blind. But certainly not as pets.'

'What about old people who enjoy them as companions?' she asked. 'Or those with heart conditions? It's medically proven that dogs and cats—any animal you can stroke, in fact—help decrease tension.' Only as she saw a dark eyebrow arch did she realise few eighteen-year-olds would have made such a knowledgeable statement. As she was trying to think of a cover up, the matter was taken from her hands.

'What a professional-sounding comment, Miss Redfern. Learned it from a medic boyfriend, did you?'

'Clever of you to guess.' Tessa plonked herself on the sofa. 'But he's no longer around.'

'How come?'

'He bored me. Always thinking and talking shop!'

The man opposite digested this in silence, and she glanced at him surreptitiously. On second viewing he was more devastating. He had attempted to smooth his hair, though a lock still fell forward. But the back and sides stayed slicked flat and showed the shape of his head and strongly muscled neck to excellent advantage. Though he obviously spent days poring over computer programs, he evidently worked out physically, as shown by the whipcord strength of his frame. Over six feet tall, she guessed, biting back a sigh at her own bare five feet one.

'I'm not here to talk about animals or boyfriends,' he went on, extricating a foot from a shaggy paw. 'I came about the job. I've engaged an admirable woman today, but she can't start for two months, and I wondered if you'd fill in for her?'

'You mean you'd put up with me?'

'I don't have a choice. The others were worse than you.'

'Thanks,' Tessa scowled. He really was an ill-mannered brute. 'You sure know how to flatter a woman, don't you?'

'When necessary.'

He gave a sudden grin and her heart jolted. What was happening to her? She wasn't normally susceptible to a man's good looks—never susceptible to a man, if she were honest—she was always too busy furthering her career to think of anything as time-consuming as a love-affair. Yet now, because of an enforced rest, she was weak at the knees when this man so much as smiled at her!

It was Sir Denis's fault. Because of him she was seeing a lonely and loveless future ahead of her and, through fear, was willing herself to fall for the first half-eligible man she met. From beneath her lashes she studied Patrick Harper again, conceding that he was *wholly* eligible, for he was handsome as Adonis and rich with it!

'Well,' he said into the silence, 'will you take the job temporarily or not?'

'How do you know you can trust me?'

'You have an honest face.'

He was taking the mickey out of her, but wasn't she doing the same with him, and loving every minute of it? 'Sorry, Mr Harper. I can't help you.'

'Why not? A few days ago you wanted the job.'

'I've changed my mind. I think you'd make a lousy employer.'

'What?' It was a moment before he found his voice again. 'I'll have you know *no one's* ever left me because they found me difficult.'

'I dare say you pay well.'

'Money doesn't come into it. They enjoy working for me.'

'Work—enjoyable?' She burst into laughter, bouncing on the sofa as if she were truly an eighteen-year-old.

'It will mean extra money in your pocket,' he said, naming a salary that was more than generous. 'And if you're keen to travel...'

'I am.'

'Then what's the problem?'

She could think of only one: if some of his domestic staff lived locally, they might discover who she was. 'You said I'll have to stand in for your staff, but I haven't a clue who they are or what they do.'

'There are Mr and Mrs Withers, my cook and butler; Pedro, the Spanish kitchen assistant, and two Filipino girls.'

All strangers to the district, she thought happily, and deliberated whether to carry on the act or come clean.

'For heaven's sake, stop dithering,' he ordered. 'I've work to do.'

Annoyed by his tone, she made her decision. 'I accept.'

'Good.' He rose, his narrow face expressionless. 'You'd better buy yourself a few decent things to wear.'

'Isn't it casual at the Hall?' she asked airily.

'There's a difference between casual and scruffy. And you're definitely scruffy.' Drawing a wallet from his pocket, he extracted two ten-pound notes. 'Here. This should do it.'

'Twenty pounds?' She giggled girlishly. 'That won't buy Henry a doggy coat!'

Irritably he peeled off another thirty.

'Generous, aren't you?' she sniffed.

'It's for working clothes, not dining with the Queen!'

She pocketed the money. 'I think I'll manage to find a few things in Iverton.'

'There are only two buses a day,' he warned.

'I'll drive.'

Sapphire eyes narrowed. 'You have a car?'

Tessa was ready for this one. 'Mr Anderson gave me permission to use his.'

The eyes remained narrowed, indicating incredulity.

'I'm not a liar, Mr Harper. If you don't believe me, I'll thank you to go.'

'I do believe you,' he said hastily. 'I was surprised, that's all.'

'So when do you want me to start?'

'Monday, at nine.'

'OK.' She didn't dare think of Mrs Benson's reaction, nor Uncle Martin's, when he heard. Much as he enjoyed a practical joke, he was likely to consider that this one was going too far. 'Let's drink to it,' she went on, padding barefoot to the cabinet and taking out a bottle of her godfather's brandy. 'How about this?'

Patrick Harper's silence spoke volumes, and the reason hit her like a thunderbolt. A house-sitter wasn't supposed to help herself to the owner's drink—and Napoleon brandy, at that!

'If you're worried about what Mr Anderson will say,' she gave him her sweetest smile, 'he told me to make myself at home.'

'There's a difference between making yourself at home and taking liberties.'

'You think that's what I'm doing?'

'Yes.' He crossed to the french windows. 'And I won't have a drink, thanks.'

'Are you teetotal?' she asked, waving the bottle at him.

'Let's say I prefer *not* to make myself at home,' he said over his shoulder.

'I promise you Mr Anderson won't be angry.'

'I'll wait until I've met him.'

'Suit yourself,' she shrugged, putting back the bottle and holding firmly on to Henry's collar till Patrick Harper closed the door behind him.

Only when he was out of sight did she do a little jig. He was utterly taken in by her! Apart from one or two slips, she hadn't done badly, though once she started seeing him on a daily basis it wasn't going to be so easy.

Mrs Benson was horrified when she heard Tessa's plan at breakfast the next morning. 'You're behaving like a child, Tessa. I'm surprised at you.'

'It's only a bit of fun.'

'What if you're found out?'

'Not a chance.'

'I can't imagine what Mr Anderson will say.'

'He'll laugh.'

'I doubt it. And what about the rest you're supposed to be having?'

'I'm feeling heaps better, and starting to be bored doing nothing. If Mr Harper hadn't played into my hands like this I'd probably have returned to work.'

'Don't be silly,' Mrs Benson said. 'You're far from well.'

Tessa flashed her most winning smile. 'Then humour me by keeping my identity secret.'

'From everyone?'

'Absolutely.'

'I still don't like what you're doing,' Mrs Benson sighed. 'When do you start?'

'Monday.'

'For how long?'

'He said two months.'

'Two months?' Mrs Benson was horrified. 'You can't keep up the joke that long.'

'I don't intend to. Only until he makes a few more asinine remarks to me. Then I'll confess and watch him squirm with embarrassment.'

'Be careful *you* aren't the one doing the squirming. Jokes can backfire, young lady.'

'This one won't.' Tessa glanced at her watch. 'I'm going into Iverton to buy a few clothes.'

'You'll do better in London.'

'I want teenage gear, not high fashion.'

'Don't you dare buy any punk outfits!'

'What a great idea!'

'Tessa Redfern, if you——'

'Only a joke, Mrs B.,' Tessa cut in from the door. 'I aim to be young but respectable!'

Half an hour later found her strolling along the high street of Iverton, the nearby market town. In the past she had actually tried the teenage departments of stores, but, though the sizing was right, the styles and colours were wrong for a serious-minded surgeon.

But for the next few weeks teenage styles were exactly what she wanted, and she boldly approached a corner shop with music blaring through its front door and its window filled with the latest jeans, leather gear and miniskirts.

To her amusement, the assistant gave her a friendly wave, and Tessa responded accordingly, trying not to wince at the hideous racket assaulting her ears as she bought figure-fitting jeans, a pair of loose cotton trousers, several tank-tops, a miniskirt and other items.

Only as she was driving past the Hall on her way home did she have a momentary qualm. But she instantly dismissed it. Patrick Harper had encouraged her into this charade by his rudeness and high-handedness. Besides, there was no real harm in her joke. It was simply a bit of light-hearted fun to lessen the tedium of her enforced vacation.

CHAPTER FOUR

ON MONDAY morning Tessa dressed in her new baggy cotton trousers and loose fitting T-shirt—ideal, the shop assistant had told her, for a warm summer's day.

But, viewing her image in the antique cheval-mirror, she had serious doubts. Regardless of how young she looked, she *felt* twenty-seven, and distinctly uncomfortable in this Charlie Chaplin outfit. Doffing it, she changed into a denim miniskirt and white cotton sweater. True, the skirt showed a lot of shapely leg, but at least she didn't feel freakish.

'Bit short, that skirt, don't you think?' Mrs Benson remarked as Tessa came into the kitchen for breakfast.

'For Miss Redfern, surgeon,' Tessa grinned, 'but not for Mr Harper's Jill-of-all-trades.'

'I wish you'd drop the whole idea. There's no telling where it will end.'

'With a laugh all round. Stop worrying, Mrs B. If the joke starts going sour, I'll end it.'

Only as she walked up the drive to the Hall did the enormity of what she was doing hit her. Thinking of the fun it might be was one thing, but acting it out was another. Still, she wasn't a Redfern for nothing, and the worst that could happen was Patrick Harper quickly seeing through her game and sending her packing.

There were half a dozen cars parked outside the main entrance, and, skirting them, she went up the stone steps to the massive oak front door. The cars signified the Hall was occupied, and she was pleased, for there was nothing worse than a fine old mansion falling into disuse.

As she went to tug the handle of the old-fashioned bell, she noticed the door ajar, and stepped inside. She had only been here once, many years ago, and remembered it as being large and gloomy. But now the gloom was a thing of the past. The oak panelling had been sanded and lightened, revealing the beauty of the wood, while the dark, tapestried chairs—given new life by expert cleaning—glowed like green, gold and red jewels in the light pouring in through the immense window halfway up the sweeping staircase. There were additions too: a magnificent glass chandelier hung from the vaulted ceiling, sparkling as it caught the sunlight coming through the open double doors that gave access to a large, rectangular drawing-room. Here, too, changes were much in evidence.

Tessa recalled the room as being dark and dreary, but today it might have come from *House and Garden*. Rag-rolled walls in delicate Wedgwood green sported excellent turn-of-the-century paintings, their predominant colours echoed in the check silk fabric covering the half dozen sofas and numerous armchairs dotted around the fully carpeted floor. It was the carpet she liked least. Thick, and soft apple-green, it reminded her of a plush medical waiting-room. None the less, she appreciated its practicality, for this part of the house must for the most part be used by the 'think-tank', whose voices and treads would have resounded alarmingly on uncarpeted floors.

She longed to explore further, but now wasn't the time, and she remained where she was, waiting for someone to appear.

'Miss Redfern?'

She swung round to the cool, faintly accented voice, and saw a statuesque blonde with a voluptuous figure appraising her from icy blue eyes.

'Yes, I'm Miss Redfern,' Tessa said, dropping her outstretched hand. 'And you are ... ?'

'Ingrid Mortensen, Mr Harper's assistant. Will you come to my office, please?'

Snooty bitch! Tessa thought, following her into a room that, for all its warm, wood antiques and thick-piled carpeting, was as cold and unwelcoming as its occupant. Even the one and only indoor plant was rigid and disciplined. Yes, 'disciplined' was an apt description of Ingrid Mortensen, Tessa concluded, noting the controlled features and silver-blonde hair impeccably coiled on the long white neck. With precise movements Ingrid went unhurriedly to her desk, adjusting the pleats of her cream linen skirt before sitting.

'I understand Mr Harper's explained what your duties are?'

'Sort of,' Tessa said, feeling suddenly ridiculous in her sweater and miniskirt beside this self-contained, exquisitely groomed young woman.

'You don't sound very certain.'

She's trying to intimidate me, Tessa thought, and set about acting her new role. 'He did tell me, but he was a bit vague. I suppose most boffins *are* when it comes to practical things,' she giggled.

'Mr Harper is never vague.'

'He was to me. Rattled on about my standing in for any staff who were off sick. But he didn't go into details.'

Ingrid's well-shaped but thin mouth thinned even more, though it in no way detracted from her spectacular beauty. 'Then I'll have to go through everything with you. This house has to run like clockwork. We can't tolerate sloppiness.'

Oh, can't we? Tessa thought stroppily, resolving that as soon as this interview was over she'd say, Thank you very much, but I've decided against working here, and walk out. This charade was meant to be fun, and if Ingrid Mortensen was going to be in charge of her it would be a disaster. Yet had she honestly expected a dynamic man to bother himself with domestic trivia? Patrick Harper might have bestirred himself to do the interviewing—perhaps he enjoyed putting his finger in everyone's personal pie—but, now that he had engaged her, it was logical to relegate her to his capable, cold assistant!

' . . . see things run smoothly,' Ingrid was saying, 'and fill in where necessary with cooking, cleaning, and——'

'A Jill-of-all-trades,' Tessa cut in brightly.

'If you wish to put it that way, yes. You do understand all I've said?'

'I'm not thick, you know—just young!'

The pale, flawless skin tinged angry pink as Ingrid rose. 'I'll take you to meet the staff.'

Silently Tessa followed her along a carpeted corridor to the large and old-fashioned kitchen. A well-scrubbed pine wood table ran down its centre, above which gleaming copper pots and pans hung from a wood beam. An enormous Aga cooker stood against one wall, with a modern electric one beside it, and a massive Welsh dresser filled with an assortment of blue and white china took up the other.

'Mr and Mrs Withers,' Ingrid said coolly, 'this is Miss Redfern.'

A pleasant-faced, middle-aged woman wiped her hands on her apron and came forward, followed by her equally pleasant-seeming husband. Tessa instantly liked them.

'Glad to have you helping us,' Mrs Withers said.

Her husband nodded, and was about to speak when Ingrid cut across him.

'I've told Miss Redfern what her duties are, so she can start right away.' Cold blue eyes examined Tessa from top to toe. 'If there's anything you need to know, please come to me. And remember this is an office as well as a home, and has to function efficiently.'

'Yes, miss.' Tessa drew herself up to her full five feet one. 'I'm here to obey your orders.'

Had she allowed a vestige of a smile to cross her face, Ingrid would have guessed she was being ribbed, but with an effort Tessa kept her features impassive, and after a moment's hesitation the girl walked out.

Only then did Tessa turn to face the older couple, pretending not to notice the amused look that passed between them. But they said nothing and she applauded their discretion, at the same time making a mental note not to allow the Swedish icicle to annoy her into losing her temper.

'What would you like me to do?' she asked Mrs Withers politely.

'Make us all a cup of tea. The minute the kettle boils, Pedro and the girls come running, and you'll meet them.'

The housekeeper was right, for no sooner had Tessa set out the cups, and the kettle started whistling, than two Filipino girls and a young Spanish boy hurried in.

Giggling, the two girls introduced themselves as Emmy and Eva, and the boy as Pedro. He spoke excellent English, and informed her his ambition was to be a cook and take over from Mrs Withers when she retired, a statement that good lady appeared to have heard umpteen times, for she nodded good-naturedly, though her husband gave him a gentle cuff on the ear and said he had a lot to learn before he was good enough to satisfy Mr Harper.

'Not that he cares what he eats when he's working on a new software idea,' Mr Withers informed Tessa. 'But when he's relaxed, he enjoys nothing better than a gourmet meal.'

'Always has done,' Mrs Withers concurred. 'Even as a little boy he loved his tummy! From the time he was a lad he'd say to me, "When I grow up and have my own house, you're going to be my very own cookie"!'

Her plump shoulders heaved with laughter, as did those of her husband, and Tessa decided there must be something innately decent about a man who inspired such devotion in this sweet couple.

'It may take you a day or two to settle in,' Mrs Withers went on, 'but once you do, you'll find the work easy.'

'What do I do with myself when there's no one to stand in for?'

'Help anyone who needs an extra pair of hands.'

'Like me,' said Emmy, jumping to her feet. 'It's time to serve the coffee.' She darted across to where the percolator was bubbling.

Shortly afterwards, Tessa helped her wheel the trolley into a light, airy room adjoining a much larger one filled with high-tech desks, chairs and the latest Harper computers.

'Food and drink aren't allowed in the computer-room,' Emmy informed her, 'and we never take the trolley in there. If a crumb gets on to a keyboard it can cause a breakdown.'

As Tessa went to reply, the members of the think-tank were upon them. She had assumed they were likely to be young, but had not anticipated their looking like first-year college students. And these were the experts devising programs that sold for hundreds—often thousands—of pounds apiece!

'I'm Billy,' a fresh-faced, tubby young man with glasses introduced himself as he took his coffee from her. 'You new around here?'

'Yes. I help out where I'm needed—except in there, of course,' she grinned, bobbing her head towards the room behind him.

'Pity,' a gangling man put in. 'I've a headache coming on and fancy a swim!'

'You'd have a bigger headache if you let me in front of your computer!'

He laughed, as did an earnest young woman with a ponytail. 'I'm Liz Cummings,' she grinned, reaching for a biscuit. 'And the would-be swimmer is my fiancé, Terry.'

In quick succession the others introduced themselves: Mike, a blond young giant, Johnny and James, thin-faced and serious-looking brothers, and a freckled-faced, sandy-haired couple who were newlyweds Tom and Jenna Donaldson.

They were a friendly, amusing bunch, and Tessa longed to learn exactly what work they did. But dutifully she asked no questions, and stood by, silent and polite, until the break was over and she and Emmy wheeled away the trolley.

She was put out to see no sign of Patrick Harper, but felt it would be too inquisitive—at this stage of her employ—to ask where he was. However, when the whole day passed without his putting in an appearance, or mention being made of him, she casually questioned Pedro, busy making pastry for an apple pie.

'He's in the States,' came the answer. 'He goes there so often we call it commuting!'

Tessa was irritated by the disappointment she felt at not seeing him. Heavens, what was special about Patrick Harper? As if she didn't know!

'Will he be away long?'

'Hard to say. Perhaps a few days, often a few weeks.'

This gave Tessa food for thought, and she debated whether to pack in the whole thing. Yet she knew she wouldn't and that it had nothing to do with boredom, more a desire to know her neighbour better. Very much better.

At dinner, she regaled Mrs Benson with the domestic details of the Hall, and though she made that good lady laugh with her impersonation of snooty Ingrid it was clear the housekeeper was still perturbed.

'I wish I weren't going on holiday tomorrow,' she grumbled. 'I don't like this silly game you're playing on innocent folk. At least if I'm here I can keep an eye on you.'

'I won't do anything to embarrass Uncle Martin,' Tessa reassured her. 'Anyway, if you don't take your holiday he'll think I'm really ill and will rush home.'

Appreciating the truth of this, Mrs Benson sighed. 'One important thing I did today,' she confided, 'was find the perfect place to keep Henry safely locked up.'

'Seems a shame to do that in such lovely weather,' Tessa said.

'He won't be shut inside. I was thinking of that fenced-off piece of grass next to the kitchen garden, where we kept him until your uncle trained him not to eat the plants. I put him in there this afternoon, and once he saw his old kennel he settled down like a lamb.'

Tessa was relieved that Henry could no longer make a nuisance of himself at the Hall, and as soon as Mrs Benson departed for the station the next morning she caught him by the collar and marched him to the enclosure.

He bounded so happily into the fenced-off area that her qualms at leaving him all day vanished. She'd pop back frequently to see him, and was delighted he didn't object to his new quarters.

For the next few days Tessa learned all about the running of the Hall, and soon appreciated why Patrick Harper elected to use it as his home and personal office.

He and his think-tank were the brains of the company, and, to ensure it remained ahead of its competitors, it was important for them to totally concentrate on what they were doing. For this, they required freedom from the hassle of an office or factory environment. And what better place in which to find peace and quiet than a lovely mansion in the countryside, impeccably run?

On her third day, Tessa took over Eva's duties, and as she dusted rooms, vacuumed carpets and changed bedlinen she felt she had discarded her surgeon's skill for that of a housemaid! Yet it was undeniably restful to know she wasn't concerned with the well-being of patients, and quite frequently a life-or-death situation, and that the worst that could happen was a broken ornament, the washing-machine's breaking down or some other domestic trivia.

She found more than enough time to pop in and out of Greentrees to check all was well, particularly with Henry, who remained extraordinarily amenable to being fenced in all day. But then he had a wonderful nature— like Uncle Martin. In fact he was so like her godfather— the way he bounded up to her, all mussed and happy to see her—that she felt they were cast in the same mould!

On her fourth day she took Pedro's place—it being his day off—and spent the morning cleaning silver and sorting out the china-room. This was a ten-foot-square area filled with Dresden, Meissen and Wedgwood dinner and tea services, to say nothing of beautiful ornaments too numerous to be displayed—unless one wished to turn the Hall into a museum rather than a home.

To her surprise she was exhausted when she returned to Greentrees each night, and by the end of the week she realised she still had a long way to go before she was well enough to tackle a full day's operating.

Despondently she made herself an omelette—having refused supper at the Hall—then went to bed. She rarely suffered the blues, yet tonight felt gloom envelop her as she saw her whole life stretching ahead of her like a lonely road, unless she met a man she loved enough to share it with—and who loved her in return! Not easy, considering the long working hours she kept.

It might be less of a problem if she fell for another surgeon, as Sir Denis had said. Except that if their schedules were different they might never get to see each other! Mocking blue eyes filled her vision, and she wondered how amenable Patrick Harper would be towards a wife who followed her own demanding career. Despite his being irritated by her casual approach to life, and urging her to train for a worthwhile job, when it came to his personal choice he might opt for a woman who centred her existence around him!

Her gloom intensified and, as if to parallel it, she heard a whine outside her bedroom door. Henry! He was given the run of the house at night and usually slept curled up on his duvet in the hall. But Tessa was the light of his doggy eyes, and whenever she was home he liked nothing better than to sleep at the foot of her bed.

Padding over to the door, she let him in. At once a shaggy bundle of fur hurled itself at her, nearly bowling her over, and a long pink tongue dedicated itself to washing her face.

'Henry, stop it!' Pushing him away, she returned to bed. But as she settled back on the pillow she found Henry staring soulfully into her eyes. His face was level with hers, his wet nose sniffing her delicately.

'You are not, definitely *not* sleeping on my bed,' she said sharply.

Big brown eyes continued to stare dejectedly into amber ones, then, recognising the voice of authority, Henry padded to the foot of the bed and settled himself on the rug.

Tessa spent an idle Saturday and Sunday, but Monday found her taking her usual route through the gap in the garden wall. It was another lovely day, and the smell of the grass, still damp with dew, and the profusion of roses scenting the flower-beds, lifted her spirits.

They rose further when she found it was Emmy's day off and she was detailed to tidy the west wing, Patrick Harper's private quarters. This must mean he was soon returning—perhaps he was already winging his way over the Atlantic!

Standing in the panelled hall, a smaller replica of the main one, she saw why he had made this his personal domain. Not only was it secluded from the rest of the house, but there was no problem in partitioning off an acre of garden. A large pool gleamed blue among the green, and luxurious poolside chairs and tables were ranged on the flagstoned surround.

Curiously she peered into the five guest suites, each with its own bathroom, then went through the dining-room, sitting-room and study. All seemed to be furnished with antiques and carpets from the main house, though she guessed the curtains to be new. But their colours were subtle and they blended in perfectly with the tranquil atmosphere.

Only the main bedroom was modern, as befitted a young tycoon of the twentieth century. Starkly dark brown, it was relieved by clever flashes of tangerine and green—in the tie-backs that held the chocolate-brown satin curtains in place, in the fabric covering the two easy chairs by the window, and the scatter cushions on a bed too large to be king-size. More likely emperor-size!

It was all too easy to visualise its owner lying in it, and, angered by her thoughts, she hurried into the dressing-room—large enough to be a bedroom in itself— and collected an armful of brown satin bed-sheets. She set about making the bed—no easy task when you were five feet one and the area you were covering seemed the size of a baseball pitch!

Puffed from the exertion, she perched on the edge to recover her breath, then nearly expired on hearing a sarcastic voice behind her.

'Make yourself at home while you're about it and have a sleep!'

Jumping to her feet, she whirled round to the tall, loose-limbed figure of her employer. No, she *hadn't* imagined the eyes blue as sapphires, the features fit for a Greek god, the body a woman could drool over... He was everything she remembered and more!

'Emmy off?' he enquired, coming close enough for her to see the faint lines of fatigue around his eyes.

'Yes, and I'm——'

'I know.' Impatiently he slipped off his jacket and undid his tie.

In normal circumstances, this wouldn't have fazed her, but his bedroom lent the action an intimacy that stifled her and made it hard to breathe. Averting her eyes from the cream silk shirt fitting snugly over the wide shoulders, she bent to the bed and tucked in the bottom sheet.

'I bet you didn't learn to do *that* in a squat!' he said.

'Learn what?' Surprised, she glanced round, and saw him nod towards the precise envelope corners she had made—a subconscious emulation of the way it was done in hospital.

'Oh *that*!' she mumbled, thinking fast. 'My girlfriend taught me. She—er—she works in a hospital.'

'A worthwhile profession. You should consider it.'

'I'm happy as I am.'

An eyebrow quirked. 'Funny little thing, aren't you?'

Her hackles rose. She hadn't been called that since medical school. 'My size is no concern of yours, and I'll thank you not to be personal.'

'You're uptight at being tiny?'

'I...am...not...tiny,' she stated in precise tones. 'I'm five feet one inch tall, which is a perfectly normal height to be. How would you like it if I referred to you as a funny tall thing?'

'It wouldn't bother me in the least. Nor would it bother *you* if you led a more meaningful life.'

'Don't you think a person can be happy drifting? Just because *you're* obsessed with work, it doesn't mean we all have to be. Now, if you'll leave me to finish your room...'

'Why should I leave?'

'Because you make me nervous.' She threw the billowy duvet—chocolate-brown with tangerine and blue piping—across the bed. 'I can't work properly with you watching me.'

'Well, if you promise not to watch *me*,' he replied, keeping his face expressionless as he unbuttoned his shirt, 'I'll change into jeans and sweater and go.'

Quick as lightning Tessa streaked to the door—acting more like a frightened virgin than a woman used to seeing nude bodies. Except she wasn't acting! The very notion of seeing Patrick Harper undressed robbed her of logic, and she was desperately frightened—not of him, but of herself, of having to acknowledge that she had finally encountered a man who made her feel vulnerable, open to hurt and disillusion. As long as she was heart-free it was easy to control her life. The moment her happiness depended on a man...

'Hey!' he called. 'I was only kidding. Come back and finish the bed.'

'I have.'

Smartly she whipped out and closed the door, almost knocking smack into Ingrid. 'Whoops!' she gasped. 'Sorry.'

'So you should be.'

'Did I hurt you? I'm awfully——'

'I'm not talking about your exit,' Ingrid hissed, 'but your stupidity in not leaving the room when Mr Harper's there. I thought I made it clear he wasn't to be bothered with stupid chatter. His ideas are worth millions and you are not to interrupt his thoughts.'

'I wasn't.' Tessa suddenly wondered if Ingrid had eavesdropped outside the door. '*He* was talking to *me*. You can ask him if you like.'

'Mr Harper's too kind to get you into trouble.'

'You must be joking!'

Too late, Tessa realised it wasn't the answer a genuine employee would have made. Yet Ingrid, for all her airs, was an employee too—which put them on a par—and Tessa wasn't going to be intimidated by her. Stretching herself to her full height, she stared up haughtily at Ingrid's five feet eight.

'I'm fully aware that you're Mr Harper's assistant, but when he engaged me he didn't inform me I'd have to report to *you*, so you've no right ordering me around.'

Angry colour swamped Ingrid's porcelain-pink skin. 'How dare you talk to me like that, you—you little nothing?'

'I'm as polite to you as you are to me,' Tessa declared, and stalked off.

Only as she returned to the main house did her anger abate sufficiently for her to regret her loss of temper. If Ingrid went running to Patrick Harper over this, her job as Girl Friday might well end this Tuesday!

CHAPTER FIVE

AT NINE-THIRTY the next morning, Tessa was left in no doubt that Ingrid had complained to Patrick, for he stormed in on her as she was clearing the remains of breakfast from the dining-room.

'I've enough to do without listening to Ingrid complaining about you,' he snarled.

'Complaining?' Tessa widened her eyes.

'Don't pretend innocence.'

'Oh, that!' Tessa said airily.

'That,' he stated, 'happens to be exactly what's made her furious. Get one thing straight, will you? Ingrid's my assistant and has full permission to give you orders. If you can't accept them, you'll have to go.'

Was this fate warning her to leave while she was still heart-free? Yet knowing how pleased Ingrid would be if she went was enough to decide her to stay. Besides, Patrick was a man like any other, and, though devilishly sexy, might become less attractive on better acqaintance! And the less she liked him, the better for her peace of mind.

'I'm sorry I'm a nuisance, sir. I won't let it happen again. I'll do everything she tells me and——'

'Don't overplay the act,' he cut in drily.

'Act?' Tessa went scarlet. How long had he known, and why had he waited till now before admitting it?

'Yes, act,' he repeated. 'I'm aware you've no respect for authority, so don't kid me you're capable of being subservient.'

She breathed easier, then said curiously, 'You *prefer* me to be subservient?'

Head on one side, he surveyed her, eyebrows drawn together. 'You couldn't be, even if you tried. And no, I don't want you to be.'

'Thanks.' She flashed him a wide smile.

'But that doesn't mean you can disregard Ingrid's orders. If she asks you to do something, do it.'

And did the Swedish girl lay it on! Over the next few days she gave Tessa as many tedious tasks as possible, from sweeping the gravel forecourt to clearing out the four-car garage, from polishing windows to weeding flower-beds!

'I wasn't told I'd have to stand in for the gardener,' Tessa protested, having finally had enough.

'You don't,' Ingrid conceded, pink-tipped fingers smoothing her silky blonde hair. 'I merely thought you'd like to be helpful.'

There was no answer to that, and Tessa vowed that next time this Swedish sadist found her another unreasonable task she'd tell her where to put it! Of course, it didn't require a genius to figure out that Ingrid was doing this to keep her out of Patrick Harper's orbit!

So successful was Ingrid that Tessa saw nothing of him for the next two days, and, since her purpose was to pull the wool over his eyes and watch his face when she finally lifted it, she debated whether to drop her little game and walk out.

'You're very pensive,' a cheerful voice broke in on her musing, and Tessa saw Mike, the blond giant from the think-tank, barring her way in the corridor. 'How are you finding things?' he went on.

'With difficulty.'

He laughed. 'People or tasks?'

'Both.'

'I'm sure you can hold your own.'

'I try.'

'Finished your work, Tessa?'

Irritation coursed through her as she swung round to see Ingrid. 'As a matter of fact, yes. I've a spare hour.'

'Then enjoy it without disturbing other people.'

'If that's a dig at me,' Mike intervened equably, 'I was giving myself a breather. Or is that against the rules?'

'Of course not.' Ingrid's tone was softer, her attitude conciliatory. 'It's simply that our little Tessa loves to chatter, which can be rather disturbing.'

Tessa fumed at this description of herself, but refused to give Ingrid the satisfaction of knowing it. 'You're quite right,' she said artlessly. 'I hope I'll have learned more sense by the time I'm your age.'

Ingrid's pale skin suffused with colour, and, turning on her heel, she stalked off.

'Beats me why she has to be unpleasant,' Mike murmured as soon as she was out of sight.

'The poor thing can't help it!' Tessa was cheeky as a teenager might be.

'Even so, she seems to have her knife into you.'

It was a pity Patrick hadn't noticed it. But then he relied on Ingrid. Maybe more than relied. It was an idea Tessa found disagreeable, yet it might account for the girl's airs and graces. Graces? Heavens, a boa constrictor was more gracious!

'Let's forget Ingrid,' Mike went on. 'It's more fun talking about you. Now, where were we?'

'I don't know where *you* were, but I'm off to give my dog a drink. I forgot to fill his bowl before I left home this morning.'

Mike groaned. 'You're putting your dog before *me*?'

'Naturally!' Tessa moved away. 'And don't say another word about him or I'll come back and bite you.'

'Is that a promise or a threat?' he called.

Laughing, she went out across the lawn, and was bending to scramble through the gap in the wall—she really must remind someone to fix it—when a cold, wet nose went smack into hers. Henry!

She reached for him, but he was too fast for her, and went tearing across the grass to the west wing. That was all she needed! Straightening fast, she ran after him, and found him sniffing and pawing outside the french windows of Patrick's private sitting-room.

'Oh, no, you don't,' she muttered, grabbing him by the collar and tugging him away. No mean feat, for he was obstinate as a mule and practically the same size. 'How did you get out, Henry? I'm positive I bolted the gate.'

A few moments later she discovered the answer, for the gate was hanging by its hinges. 'Naughty boy,' she scolded sternly, at the same time admiring his tenacity.

Sensing it, he barked and wagged his tail, then tried to pull away from her restraining hand.

'Not this time, bud. You're Henry, not Houdini, and I'm going to make good and sure you don't escape again.'

Uttering the magic word 'Food', she managed to propel him into the kitchen, and, leaving him happily munching biscuits, she raided the garden shed for stout wire and wire-cutters.

It took her the best part of half an hour to secure the gate sufficiently for Henry not to break it open again, and to return him to his enclosure. Raising beseeching eyes at her, he whined pitifully, and Tessa, whose heart normally melted at this, determinedly walked back to the Hall. She had been away long enough and didn't fancy giving Ingrid an excuse to lambaste her.

Once again she wondered why the girl was jealous of her. After all, an eighteen-year-old drop-out was hardly competition for a sophisticated Swedish beauty. Yet the scene with Mike illustrated her bitterness and frustration. But frustration at what?

The answer was clear: at not getting to first base with Patrick!

Musing on this, she wondered if he made it a rule not to mix business with pleasure. Or did he genuinely not fancy the girl? Though she was beautiful enough to interest most men, her aloof attitude might have turned him off. Except she was anything but aloof with him...

Intrigued to learn more about her, Tessa resolved to pump Mrs Withers, and her chance came soon after lunch, when she stayed behind for another cup of tea.

'Ingrid's background?' the woman echoed Tessa's question. 'Far as I remember she comes from a village in Sweden, though she never talks about her family. Why the curiosity?'

'I was trying to figure out why she's sharp with everyone.'

'Ask her!'

'She'd eat me for breakfast!'

Mrs Withers chuckled and handed Tessa a knife. 'Vent your curiosity on the tomatoes. Put them in boiling water for a few minutes and then skin them.'

Just what I'd like to do to Ingrid! Tessa thought, switching on the kettle. Next time I find her snooping on me I'll walk out.

An hour later, she was placing a vase of fresh flowers on Patrick's desk, it being Emmy's day off, when he strode in.

'Always underfoot,' he said half jokingly. 'One day I'll open a cupboard and find you popping out!'

'Don't you like flowers?' she asked, continuing to arrange them.

'I like peace and quiet better.'

'I'm only doing my job, as a Girl Friday should.'

'You seem to be a Monday, Tuesday, Wednesday and Thursday one as well,' he grunted.

'Then I'll take the flowers away.' Crossly she reached for the vase, her hand sending the crystal paperweight teetering on the edge of the desk.

'Watch out!' He lunged past her and caught it. 'Talk about clumsy! You're a real butter-fingers!'

'How right you are,' she said, hiding a smile at the thought of his seeing her in the operating theatre!

'Am I interrupting?' Ingrid's cool voice enquired from the doorway.

Tessa's smart reply died on her lips as she remembered her role. 'I knocked over the crystal paperweight, but Mr Harper saved it.'

'Did you want me, Ingrid?' Patrick asked her.

'Only to tell you Mr Allinson and his directors are arriving at seven,' she said in the dulcet tones she reserved for him, 'and that I've arranged dinner for eight-thirty.'

'I wish I'd never let you talk me into inviting them,' he muttered. 'I can't raise the capital to go into partnership with Allinson, and he's too tough to let me buy into his company below the market price.'

'I think you should settle for a twenty-five per cent share.'

'Forget it. If his equity is more than mine, he'll order me around. Either I go in with him on equal terms, or I go it alone.'

'If you sold this house you'd have the money you want.'

'I'd still be half a million pounds short.'

'Surely not? The land will fetch——'

'I'm not selling to developers. They'd flood the district with bungalows and ruin the environment for miles around.' Patrick placed a strong, well-shaped hand on her shoulder. 'I recognise you've my best interests at heart, Ingrid, but, much as I'd like to link up with Allinson Software, my conscience won't let me do it that way.'

'You and your conscience,' she sniffed, though the faint smile that softened her delicately shaped mouth reminded Tessa that even a glacier could melt under a strong-enough sun.

But why am I listening to these two talking business? she asked herself, and sidled to the door.

'I want to talk to you, Tessa,' Ingrid called. 'I assume you can wait at table?'

'Why?'

'Because Emmy won't be back till late.'

'Can't Eva take her place?' Tessa had never waited at table in her life, and was worried she'd make a hash serving a dinner that was obviously an important one.

'No, she can't. She'll be helping in the kitchen.'

'What about Pedro?' Tessa said desperately. 'There are masses of Spanish waiters!'

'I'm sure there are. But Pedro isn't one of them. He happens to have two left hands, which only leaves you.'

'You've never done waitressing before?' Patrick teased, his humour restored. 'I thought it was a standby for out-of-work girls.'

'I've never been unemployed,' Tessa retorted, fully back in her guise. 'I *chose* not to work!' His expression was so pained by the very idea that she embroidered on it. 'Most people only do it for the money. Me, I manage fine on the dole.'

'Then why are you house-sitting for Mr Anderson?' Ingrid enquired, a hostile gleam in her eyes.

'I need the extra cash to travel around Europe. And having this job as well will let me do it in style.'

'If you hope to continue having this job,' Ingrid replied bitingly, 'put on Emmy's uniform and help Withers set the table for dinner.'

'You're the boss,' Tessa said airily, and went in search of Eva, who gave her one of Emmy's dresses.

Luckily Emmy was as slim as Tessa, though the skirt came to her ankles, and soon after she'd helped Withers in Patrick's private dining-room she hurried home to put a few tucks in the dress, return Henry to the house and give him his supper.

He was less than pleased when she left him again, and his howl of displeasure was ringing in her ears as she made her way to the west wing.

She felt very self-conscious in Emmy's dress, its severe line and navy colour making her look smaller and more fragile than usual. The guests were already seated in Patrick's softly lit drawing-room, and Withers was passing round the drinks.

A grey-haired man in his fifties, and the carefully coiffured woman in sequined blue beside him, had to be John Allinson and his wife, she decided from the way Patrick—elegant in charcoal-grey suit and cream silk shirt—was giving them his undivided attention. Further down the room, Ingrid, nauseatingly beautiful in turquoise, ash-blonde hair caught back with a wide, shimmering hair-slide, acted hostess to three men—all tall, suntanned, and exuding the confident air of successful, high-powered executives.

Half an hour later they were seated around the candle-lit dining table. Silver bowls of pink roses ranged down the centre of the finely embroidered white cloth, literally sparkling with silver place-settings, gleaming china and crystal goblets. And as the meal progressed Tessa did not put a hand wrong in helping Withers serve it.

Mrs Withers had excelled herself. Her cold tomato soup was a supreme blend of tomatoes, cream and basil, while her roast lamb—which at the worst of times was excellent—was a picture of tender juiciness. Second helpings were asked for and Tessa saw her hopes of bringing Henry a meaty bone vanish.

'Don't worry,' Withers whispered to her under his breath. 'There's another leg in the kitchen for the staff and Mrs W. won't forget Henry.'

Tessa flashed him a smile, only aware she still had it on her face when she turned and saw Patrick give her a startled glance.

Instantly she composed her features, primping her mouth and moving with clockwork precision from guest to guest as she took away their plates and served the dessert—home-grown peaches marinaded in apricot liqueur and decorated with Devonshire cream.

Only as she reached Patrick's side did she notice the amused gleam in his eyes, confirmed by his saying in her ear, 'You're doing fine, Tessa. There's no need to be so solemn.'

'Thank you, sir——' She almost curtsied.

'Shall we have coffee in the drawing-room?' Ingrid's cool tones cut across the muted conversation. 'Or do you men wish to have it alone here?'

'In the drawing-room,' John Allinson answered, glancing at his wife and then Patrick. 'If I talk business without Marjorie's being present, I'll only have to repeat it to her again!'

Amid laughter, they returned to the drawing-room.

It was a perfect summer's evening, balmy and clear, and the french windows were open to the terrace and floodlit pool beyond. Conversation was general as Tessa passed round the coffee and Withers deftly proffered liqueurs and cigars.

'I think you made a wise decision moving to the countryside for your creative work,' John Allinson said, puffing contentedly on his cigar.

'It's also an excellent way of utilising a place this size,' one of the other Americans interjected.

'That's another reason for my move,' Patrick agreed. 'This west wing is more than adequate for the largest family, so the rest of the house would have stood empty.'

'Personally, I'd find working here too peaceful and quiet,' a balding, red-faced man called Hank added.

'It's not always like this,' Patrick drawled. 'There's a very disruptive dog next door who comes in and drools over me!'

'This is the perfect setting for dogs,' Mrs Allinson said brightly. 'I can just envisage bassets and beagles bounding around here, and perhaps a red setter or two. They'd be real cute on your Persian carpet.'

'A dog's place is outside,' Patrick stated.

'Surely not the whole time?'

'Not everyone is as crazy about dogs as you are, Marjorie,' her husband smiled. 'If you——'

There was a strangled bark and Tessa froze. Oh, no! Life wasn't that cruel! But it was, for Henry came gambolling around the side of the terrace in all his shaggy glory, a huge lamb-bone clamped between his teeth, and sat himself in the doorway of the drawing-room.

'Talk of the devil,' Patrick muttered.

'What a darling dog,' Mrs Allinson gushed.

At the cooing tone, Henry rose.

'Sit!' Tessa hissed as loudly as she dared. But Henry was as oblivious to her as he was to Mrs Allinson, for he had already spied his idol.

Bone held high, he pranced towards Patrick as delicately as a Lipizzaner horse, and, like a horse in a drawing-room, left mayhem behind him: sweeping tail dashing objects from low-lying tables, jowls drooling droplets on to the carpet, fat paws leaving earthy marks.

Tessa made a lunge for him, but Henry bounded forward, and she watched with horror as he reached

Patrick's side, gazed at him with doggy adoration, then slowly lowered his shaggy head to place his lamb-bone as an offering on Patrick's pristine lap.

CHAPTER SIX

FOR as long as she lived, Tessa would never forget her mortification over Henry's appalling behaviour, nor the bubble of laughter that escaped her.

Though instantly stifled, everyone heard it, and Patrick and Ingrid flung her thunderous looks before forcing smiles to their faces. Well, they had to smile, for the guests were also suppressing their laughter, albeit more successfully than Tessa had done.

'I'm sorry, Mr Harper,' she mumbled, rushing over to scoop the bone from his lap.

Anger still darkened his face, but as she watched him the humour of the situation struck him and he half smiled.

'You'll have to do something about that damned dog,' he said under his breath, picking shreds of meat from his trousers.

Tessa went to help him, then stopped, colour flaming her cheeks. Glancing up, he noticed it, and one eyebrow rose mockingly. But then why shouldn't he be amused when the joke was now on *her*?

'Isn't the dog yours, Patrick?' Mrs Allinson asked.

'It belongs next door, where I live,' Tessa came swiftly into the conversation, then glanced Patrick's way. 'Will you excuse me, sir, while I take him home?'

'I wouldn't dream of stopping you!'

As Tessa went out, dragging a reluctant Henry, the burst of laughter that came from behind her showed that Patrick had managed to retrieve a potentially embarrassing situation. And thank heavens for that, otherwise it could have ruined his evening. As it was, *she* was the one with egg on her face!

'Tessa!'

Swinging round, she saw Ingrid coming towards her, and braced herself for a tirade.

'You deserve to be fired!' the Swedish girl hissed. 'I'll discuss it with Mr Harper in the morning.'

'You can't blame me for Henry's behaviour,' Tessa defended haughtily. 'If the stone wall were mended, he wouldn't have got in here.' Nonplussed, Ingrid remained silent, a situation which Tessa took advantage of. 'Mr Harper's well aware that the roots of the cypress on *his* land caused the damage, and if he doesn't want Henry around he knows what to do.' Upon which she turned on her heel and stalked off.

Despite making out a good case for Henry, Tessa didn't feel blameless, for she must have left a door ajar for the dog to open. That was only too true, she saw the instant she entered the kitchen at Greentrees, for the back door was gaping wide.

'I must be losing my marbles,' she muttered. 'I'll have to double-check doors and windows each time I go out.'

It wasn't until next morning, when distance softened the edge of her annoyance with herself, that she fully appreciated the humour of last night's scene. Had she deliberately set out to cut Patrick down to size, she couldn't have done better, except that she didn't wish to harm him business-wise, which might have happened had he lost his temper with Henry. It was all too easy to imagine Mrs Allinson, the great dog-lover, warning her husband to have nothing to do with a man who disliked dogs! As it was, Patrick had emerged from the incident smelling of roses—as well as lamb-bone!

As she entered the Hall, Pedro sped towards her, hissing that Mr Harper wished to see her the moment she arrived. Her spirits plummeted. He was going to fire her after all. She didn't blame him. In his shoes she'd do the same. Should she disclose her identity before leaving? Yet doing it now wouldn't have the impact on him as she had planned, and she decided to keep mum.

'Is he in his office?' she asked.

'No, by the pool.'

Hurriedly she rounded the house, amazed by the misery engulfing her at the prospect of not seeing Patrick after today. Not him personally, she told herself hurriedly, but the fun of this whole charade. Glancing at the narrow denim skirt barely skimming her knees, and the white cotton top that lightly touched her delicate curves—boldly stating 'Donald Duck for President'—she realised how much she'd enjoyed shedding her serious image.

As she arrived at the pool, Patrick's lithe figure was cleaving through the sparkling blue water, legs threshing powerfully, arms moving rhythmically. Though she was in his direct line of vision, he did not acknowledge her, but finished the length and began another. Since those brilliant blue eyes of his weren't short-sighted, she sensed he was deliberately keeping her waiting, and she assumed a pose of nonchalance and settled herself on a lounger. Not that she actually lounged—that was asking for a reprimand—but she felt entitled to make herself comfortable, regardless of his lordly presence.

Patrick swam two more lengths, which suited her fine, for it was particularly pleasant sitting here on a lovely English summer's day, watching a handsome man swim back and forth in this magnificent free-form pool. More than handsome, she thought, as he hauled himself from the water in one swift movement, bronzed and gleaming except where brief black trunks clung to his body like a second skin.

'I want to talk to you,' he stated, planting himself squarely in front of her, and flinging back a lock of chestnut hair from his eyes.

'If you're referring to last night,' she said sweetly, 'it was as much your fault as Henry's.'

'Too true,' he grunted. 'The wall's being fixed.'

Reaching for the towelling robe that hung on the branch of a nearby tree, he shrugged into it, and it was an effort for Tessa to keep her eyes from the muscles rippling in his chest.

What's the matter with me? she thought irritably. I've seen hundreds of men's chests in my time, probably thousands, yet none have affected me this way. So why now? Because he's a perfect specimen of manhood, she answered herself, and my medical eye appreciates it. His chest, indeed his entire body, didn't have an ounce of superfluous flesh on it, the play of muscles beneath the golden skin indicating superb fitness.

'...not entirely to blame.'

With a start she realised he was still talking, and as she tried to guess what he had said her expression told him she hadn't a clue.

'The least you can do is listen to me,' he reproved.

'I'm sorry, I—er—I was trying to think who could mend the wall for you.'

'I've already told you it's being done,' he repeated. 'But that doesn't mean you can let that dog of yours roam free. If he does, he'll find another way of getting in here.'

'I think he fancies you!' A smile tilted her mouth provocatively, and she was instantly aware of Patrick's eyes resting there, and a sudden stillness coming over his face.

She had seen that expression on a man's face before, though not for years, due to the way she had hedged herself around with work, with no time for anything else. But now there was all the time in the world. Well, six

weeks at least, and it might be fun if she... Watch it!
she warned herself. Don't start anything you'll regret.

'Henry isn't used to being locked up,' she said aloud.
'Mr Anderson believes animals should be free.'

'How come you're so knowledgeable about Mr
Anderson?'

'From his housekeeper,' Tessa said hurriedly. 'She also
says the reason Henry likes you is because you remind
him of his last owner. The company he works for sent
him to Egypt for three years, and he gave him to Mr
Anderson.'

'I can't believe anyone would want to give Henry
away,' Patrick commented sarcastically, settling himself
on a lounger. 'But enough of that dog.' Blue eyes ap-
praised her. 'You did Emmy's job very well last night.
Withers said you were quite professional. I'm sure I can
find you work in a restaurant when you leave here.'

'Waitressing?' she screeched, shaking her head. 'I've
more respect for my feet!'

'You'd earn good money.'

'Forget it. It sounds dead boring.'

'You seem to find everything boring.'

'Maybe I won't when I'm your age,' she said, biting
back a laugh at his indignant expression. 'Sorry, Mr
Harper, I didn't mean to offend you.'

'I appreciate your viewpoint, Tessa. What are you—
seventeen, eighteen? As I said, I'm almost old enough
to be your father.'

'Don't be silly. You're fit and healthy and don't look
a day over thirty!'

'What a compliment!' His tone was dry as hay. 'But
to get back to you—you're not seriously thinking of
bumming round Europe, are you?'

'Have you a better suggestion? And don't say you see
me as a high-powered businesswoman!'

'Never that!'

'A teacher, then?'

'You're bossy enough to be one, but no.'

She pursed her lips. 'What about a doctor?'

He burst out laughing. 'Heaven help your patients. You're not doctor material, I'm afraid. You're too——'

'If you say "small",' she cut across him, 'I'll throw up!'

'But it's true.' His eyes roamed her. 'Perfectly formed, but small. Why not accept it instead of denying it?'

'I don't deny it. I merely think size has nothing to do with performance.'

'*That's* for sure,' he said drily.

Aware he had found a double meaning in her comment, she went scarlet.

'Sorry,' he apologised. 'I forgot how young and innocent you are.'

'Eighteen-year-olds aren't innocent these days,' she came back at him. 'You're showing your age!'

'So it appears.'

'Anyway, I haven't yet decided if I'm going to travel. I might surprise you by taking up a profession.'

'Fine. As long as it doesn't prevent your marrying and having a family,' he said.

Tessa was astonished. Was he teasing? Yet his expression didn't suggest it. 'Why will work stop me doing that?' she asked. 'Plenty of high-powered women marry and have children.'

'And plenty put their career before a personal life.'

Tessa swallowed hard, silently conceding she was one of them, and vowing to change. 'Women are often forced to put their career first when they're trying to establish themselves,' she defended. 'But once they have——'

'They're generally too set in their ways—often too hard-boiled—for the give and take of a relationship.'

'Don't give me that "generally" bit,' Tessa said crossly. 'I know masses of women who hold excellent jobs yet also manage to have children, run a home and have a happy marriage.'

'Do you?' Patrick asked sarcastically. 'I wasn't aware you mixed in such circles.'

Tessa thought fast. 'I'm perfectly capable of reading, and women's magazines are full of such stories.'

'That's exactly what they are,' he snorted. 'Fiction!'

'If you're going to joke about it,' she sniffed, 'there's no point talking. But I'll say one thing more. I met a woman doctor in London who has a big practice, a large house, four kids and a happy husband!'

'She's an exception.'

Exasperated, Tessa glared at him. 'Are you always pig-headed?'

'I beg your pardon?'

'Sorry,' she mumbled. 'I meant obstinate.'

The firm mouth curled in a supercilious smile. 'I'm neither obstinate nor pig-headed. Merely a realist.' He lay back in the lounger and folded his hands behind his head, his expression shuttered.

'Does that mean you won't marry a career woman?' she found herself asking. Mrs Withers had said as much, but Tessa wished to hear it from the horse's mouth, so to speak.

'Got it in one!' he stated emphatically. 'When and if I give up my freedom, I'll want to be the centre of the lady's life.'

Tessa searched his face for a glint of humour, but his eyes and mouth were deadly serious, and disappointment that he was so narrow-minded engulfed her.

'Wipe that accusation off your face,' he stated. 'I'm only telling you what most men want. Unfortunately they haven't the guts to say it, or the strength of mind to stick to it. They fall in love and their intelligence goes walkabout! Not that I'd want a complete homebody. Merely a woman who'll love me enough to make my life hers.'

'You must introduce me to this paragon when you find her,' Tessa said.

'I haven't yet started searching. I enjoy my freedom too much to think of curtailing it.' He yawned and stretched, the gesture drawing her eyes to his flat stomach, and the narrow line of dark hair that disappeared into the figure-hugging swimming-trunks.

With an effort she tried to view him dispassionately, as a surgeon, yet only saw him with the eyes of a woman—a woman who was uncomfortably aware of her femininity, of the years going by too fast, of the children she wanted to have, the passion she wanted to share. Hurriedly, she turned and walked away.

'You look as if you've had a set-to with Mr Harper,' Withers commented as she entered the kitchen.

'He annoyed me by making stupid remarks about career women.'

'Why does that bother you?' Mrs Withers came into the conversation with a chuckle. 'You're not likely to be one!'

'Maybe not. But I never imagined he was old-fashioned.'

'He was teasing you.'

Tessa was on the verge of saying she didn't think so when Withers spoke to his wife.

'Don't forget Miss Rogers.'

'Ah, yes.'

Tessa's ears pricked up. 'Who's Miss Rogers?'

Mrs Withers hesitated, reluctant to gossip, and Tessa gave the woman her most winning smile, which did the trick.

'She was a close friend of Mr Patrick's. An interior decorator. That's how he met her—when she designed his office. We all thought *she'd* be the one.' Mrs Withers' tone made it quite clear what she meant. 'But then she was offered a job decorating some sheikh's palace in the Middle East, and accepted it.'

'What was wrong with that?'

'It meant her being away six months. In my day, a woman had more sense. Mr Patrick was real mad.'

'Hurt,' Withers corrected. 'There's a difference, my dear.'

'Six months isn't long,' Tessa defended the unknown Miss Rogers.

'She'd probably have gone off again when another job came her way,' Mrs Withers added.

'You think she should have given up her career, then?'

'I think she could have found enough work to keep her in England.'

'Why is it always the woman who has to sacrifice her career because of the man she loves?' Tessa questioned crossly.

'Because it's usually easier for a woman, and it was certainly easier in Miss Rogers' case.'

'I'd never jeopardise *my* career for a man.'

'Wait till you fall in love,' Mrs Withers said.

'Wait till you *have* a career,' Mr Withers added, a comment which successfully stopped Tessa in her tracks.

CHAPTER SEVEN

TESSA'S conversation with Patrick, and her subsequent one with Mr and Mrs Withers, gave her food for thought, and highly indigestible it was too.

Mulling it over as she returned to Greentrees at mid-morning to feed Henry, she admitted that, though she now realised she wanted a husband and family, she hadn't even considered what an upheaval marriage would make in her life, having largely assumed everything would automatically fall into place. Yet things didn't fall into place unless they were arranged properly, and this meant making it clear to the man who shared her life that her patients were a very important part of it.

Of course the mythical man of her recent dreams had understood this, but how would a real-life man act? Someone like Patrick, for example?

No need for conjecture there! He'd made his opinion abundantly clear. She was almost tempted to march back and tell him exactly who she was. Except he'd then guess how furious he had made her. And she was darned if she'd let him know that!

Greentrees came in sight, and she hurried the last few yards to the front door. As she opened it, she tensed. Someone was here. Her scalp prickled and she edged backwards, not sure whether to run or scream. Steps sounded above her head and her hand reached for the doorknob.

'Is that *you*?' called a warm voice.

Tessa's breath came out in a gasp as Mrs Benson appeared at the top of the stairs. 'I thought you were a burglar! I wasn't expecting you back yet.'

'It didn't stop raining, and I also kept worrying what you were doing.'

'Having fun.'

'At that poor man's expense.'

'He has his money's worth out of me,' Tessa defended. 'Anyway, I'll probably give it up in a week.' She edged to the door. 'See you later.'

'Why the hurry? You've just got here.'

'I only came to find out if everything was OK. But it's not necessary now you're here.'

Returning to the Hall, Tessa unexpectedly felt deflated. Maybe she'd make Mrs Benson happy and end her charade this afternoon. She'd set out the tea things, then take the bull by the horns and confess all to Patrick. Well, not all, and maybe not today—she didn't quite have the courage. Heavens, what a muddle she had got herself into!

She was reflecting on this as she sat alone in the kitchen—Emmy having wheeled out the tea trolley—when Patrick strolled in.

'I'm hungry,' he announced.

'Emmy has a chocolate cake on the trolley.'

'I'm talking of proper food.' He sat opposite her. 'I missed lunch.'

About to ask why, Tessa remembered the think-tank was devising software for an international engineering company, and the staff were under orders not to ask it to stop for meals, but leave the heated trolleys in the main dining-room for people to help themselves. But Patrick often worked in the west wing, existing on fruit, and coffee from a thermos, until he'd solved what he was working on.

'It's bad for the gastric juices not to eat regular meals,' she said, going to the refrigerator and taking out a tureen of iced cucumber soup.

'Don't bother with a plate,' he said.

'Are you going to have all of it?'

'I'm starving.'

'Then have a proper meal.'

'Bossy little thing, aren't you?'

Recognising he was trying to rile her, she felt no annoyance. 'Ingrid's bossy, and she's tall as a beanpole.'

'A willow,' Patrick corrected, amused. 'You don't like her, do you?'

'It's mutual.' Tessa set the tureen in front of him.

'That's a pretty watch.'

Startled, she glanced at her wrist, heart racing as she saw the gold Rolex Uncle Martin had given her on her twenty-fifth birthday. Since working here she hadn't worn it, but this morning must have automatically put it on.

'You'd never think it was a copy,' she said brightly. 'Looks like the real thing, doesn't it?'

'It certainly does.'

Anxious for him not to regard it too closely, she swung round to the sink and busied herself there.

'Getting back to Ingrid,' he said unexpectedly, 'it's part of her job to see everything here runs smoothly, and if she orders you around it's because she thinks it's necessary.'

'Is it necessary to be unpleasant?'

'It's her way. She's a first-class administrator and works non-stop.'

'A first-class administrator wouldn't need to!'

Patrick went to reply, then thought better of it, and Tessa hid a smile, well pleased with herself. 'Fancy cold meat and salad?'

'I'd prefer a sandwich. Peanut butter and strawberry jam.'

'Yes, sir.' Wondering if he'd dreamed up this combination to shock her, or if his taste in food was genuinely weird, she took a loaf of wholemeal bread from an earthenware crock and began slicing it. Hearing him chuckle, she glanced up. 'What's the joke?'

'Those.' He pointed to the inch-thick slices. 'You're very heavy-handed for such a little thing.'

She bit back a laugh. If he saw her in the operating theatre, he'd be grinning the other side of his face! She eyed the slices. Definitely doorsteps, but that was because her concentration had lapsed. When it came to the scalpel, though . . .

'Good girl,' he said.

'Why?'

'For controlling your temper. Normally when I refer to your size you bite my head off.'

'I may do it yet.' She slapped peanut butter and jam on the bread. 'I find you extremely irritating.'

'You don't mean that.' There was a noticeable gleam in his eye as she passed him his sandwich.

Why is he staring at me? she wondered, and turned away before he noticed the flush staining her cheeks.

'You were a bit mean with the jam,' he mumbled, mouth full.

'Sorry.' Head still averted, she reached for his plate. But it was his hand she caught, and before she had a chance to pull away she was on his lap and he was pressing his mouth to hers.

It was the first time he had touched her, and she was frighteningly conscious of every part of his body: his hands on her waist, his fingers kneading her skin in a gentle, insidious motion that sent little flames of desire shooting through her. His knees were hard beneath her own, his thighs firm against her soft buttocks, the hard wall of his chest straining against the roundness of her breasts, and his mouth, those two sensuous lips, covering hers and gently prising them open.

She made no effort to resist him, and nestled closer, enjoying the taste of him, the special aroma that signified Patrick. She felt herself being carried away on a sea of passion that threatened to engulf her, and she exulted in it, waiting for the next wave.

But the next wave didn't come. Instead, she found herself being set on her feet, and Patrick drawing away from her.

'Sorry,' he said in clipped tones, his expression half contrite, half irritated. 'I don't normally go in for cradle-snatching.'

Chilled by his swift change of mood, she felt hers change too. He might be angry with himself, but that was nothing to the anger *she* felt for him! How dared he kiss her and make her respond when he felt nothing in return? He deserved only one comment, and she let him have it.

'You don't need to feel guilty,' she said flippantly. 'I left my cradle a long while ago.'

'Oh, sure,' he said sarcastically. 'I can tell you're very experienced.'

He had caught her on the raw, though she hid it by tossing her head, as if to show he was so unimportant in her scheme of things that she hadn't bothered resisting his kiss. Come to think of it, that was the right answer to give him.

'I can't get worked up over a middle-aged man, Mr Harper, even when he's a handsome one.'

'That's understandable,' he drawled. 'I've never before fancied a teenager. I prefer my women sophisticated.'

'Like you?'

'Don't you think I am?'

She made herself laugh. 'No sophisticated man would apologise for a simple kiss. It was the kind you'd give your grandmother!'

With a strangled sound he moved towards her, stopping abruptly as Ingrid sauntered in. Amazing how the girl sensed when she and Patrick were together, Tessa thought. Did she have hidden microphones or X-ray eyes?

'Ah, Patrick,' she murmured. 'I'm glad you're eating.'

Without answering, he strode past her and out, and Tessa, expecting Ingrid to be annoyed, was surprised to find her watching his departing back almost tenderly.

'When he's working on a problem, he can't think of anything else,' the girl murmured.

Oh, yeah? Tessa thought, and derived great pleasure from silently telling Ingrid what she'd have seen if she'd come into the kitchen five minutes earlier.

'I hope you weren't bothering him with your stupid chatter,' Ingrid went on.

'I'm not sure. He was chuckling too much to tell me!'

Ingrid's mouth thinned into a hard line. 'Patrick was chuckling *at* you, not *with* you. He finds you such an interesting specimen, he said he'd like to put you in a glass jar.'

'In his bedroom?' Tessa asked, enjoying the flare of rage that crossed Ingrid's face before she turned on her heel and slammed the door behind her.

Despite her victory over the Swedish girl, Tessa wasn't happy. Patrick's kiss had awakened emotions that had lain dormant for years, and she wasn't sure she could batten them down again. It wasn't a pleasant thought for a young woman who prided herself on her control, and she sensed there was a long evening of deep thought ahead of her.

For the first time she didn't take the short cut home through the garden wall, for the gap was half closed and a pile of stones beside it was testimony to its completion tomorrow. Instead she walked down the long drive, arms swinging, and breathing deeply of the flower-scented air. She was nearing the wrought-iron gates when a car purred to a stop beside her.

'You've finished early,' Patrick said.

'Yes.' Turning her head, she stared into his blue, blue eyes, but resolutely refused to be swayed by their brilliance.

'Until tomorrow, then,' he said.

Was that a question or a statement? Instinct told her he wasn't sure if she had left because there was no more work to do, or was actually quitting.

'I won't be in tomorrow,' she stated.

'Dammit, Tessa! Do you want me to apologise again for kissing you?' He jumped from the car and took a step towards her, then thought better of it and leaned against the door. 'I told you it was an impulse and won't happen again.'

She shrugged, in two minds whether or not to do as he'd thought, and quit.

'From now on you'll be safe with me,' he assured her.

Detecting faint amusement in his voice, she knew he thought she was over-reacting. And he was right too. Were she really the eighteen-year-old hippy she was pretending to be, she'd have thought nothing of his kiss. By waxing indignant, she was acting like the inhibited twenty-seven-year-old she really was. Hard on this thought came another chastening one: the realisation that most women her age were far more experienced than *she* was.

Aware of his still leaning against the side of the car, casually elegant in black linen trousers and sweater, she felt herself responding yet again to his magnetism. 'I'll stay on,' she heard herself say.

'Good. And you have my word I'll keep my distance.'

'You'd better.' She walked past him.

'See you tomorrow,' he called.

'I told you I'm not coming in.'

'But I thought you——'

'I'm taking the day off.' It was a sudden decision, but she felt the need to put distance between herself and this man.

'Going to London?'

'Where else? It's the only place to be if you want a good time.'

'I imagine you always have a good time,' he said sourly, slipping back into the car and switching on the ignition.

She continued on her way to Greentrees, curious as to why Patrick was put out at the thought of her going to town, and wondering if he was more attracted to his teenage helper than he cared to admit!

It was an amusing thought, and it led to others that were less amusing, though considerably more interesting.

And also more dangerous.

CHAPTER EIGHT

HAVING committed herself to a day in London, Tessa resisted the urge to call on Sir Denis—aware that if she set foot in the hospital she might succumb to the temptation of returning to work—and decided instead to visit Bobby Millet, keen to discover how he was progressing with his work for the silver and wood exhibition he and a friend were mounting.

Reaching the bench under Uncle Martin's favourite oak, she perched on it. Yes, she'd visit Bobby. He always made her feel good, which couldn't be said of Patrick—and definitely not of Ingrid! Leaning against the bark, she thought back to the start of her friendship with her erstwhile patient...

An infection had set in the day after she had operated on him for peritonitis, and, looking up from examining him, she saw a broad smile on the face of this extremely ill young man.

'You can't be feeling as good as your smile,' she said.

'I'm fine,' he whispered—with a temperature of a hundred and four!

'Tell Nurse when you're in pain and she'll give you another injection.'

'It's not necessary. I'm OK.'

It was the same each time she saw him: he was always 'fine' and always cheerful. Then, a week later, when his temperature was near normal, she was greeted with, 'Hi, Doc. If you attach me to any more tubes I'll feel like a steam-engine!'

'What do you know about steam-engines?' she teased.

'Lots. They're my hobby.'

It was an unlikely hobby for a young man with dyed blond spiky hair and an earring. 'I thought they were extinct.'

'Not quite. A few are used in India and South America, and one day I plan to see every one of them.'

'That's a tall order.'

'It gives me a goal to aim at. One day I'll make my fortune and travel!'

'What do you do?'

'I make wood carvings and sell 'em in street markets.'

'I'd like to see them,' she said idly, not meaning it.

'Come to Battersea and you can. I live with two pals of mine. Ain't Buckingham Palace, but it keeps out the wet!'

A week later Bobby left hospital, and a month afterwards dropped her a note inviting her to tea. Deciding it was rude to refuse his invitation, she wrote back saying she was free next Saturday afternoon, and so found herself—on her one day off in a month—outside a decrepit Victorian house in a back street in Battersea. Her first instinct was to turn tail and run, but, taking her courage in her hands, she knocked on the battered front door.

No answer. She knocked again. Still no one came. Perhaps Bobby had forgotten she was coming and gone out?

Ah, well, she thought, descending the steps, at least I made the effort. She was walking off when the door behind her opened. Turning, she saw a leather-jacketed young man in the doorway, sporting a black coxcomb hair-do.

'You the doctor?' he questioned, giving her the once-over.

'Don't be daft,' a second young man with a rainbow-coloured frizz answered over his friend's shoulder. 'She's too young.'

'Stop it, you two,' Bobby said, coming up behind them. 'Glad you made it, Doc. Come in. Jeff, Tim, this is the lady who saved my life.'

'You wasted your time!' Jeff of the rainbow frizz informed her, and the others laughed and led Tessa into a small kitchen, where a bare wooden table was set with gaily coloured mugs and a packet of biscuits on a plate.

'Found your way OK?' Bobby beamed, pulling out a chair for her.

'First go,' she smiled, strangely at home with these young men. Punks they might be, but they were friendly as puppies!

'Come to admire Bobby's work?' asked Tim—the one with the coxcomb—cutting into her thoughts.

'What's there to admire?' Bobby cut in, bringing across the kettle.

'You're dead right,' Jeff agreed. 'You need a magnifying glass to make out some of your carvings.'

'It keeps the wolf from the door,' Bobby shrugged, passing round the biscuits.

'I'd like to see them anyway,' Tessa said politely, envisaging the little animals and gnomes one found in markets. The reality when, a half-hour later, she followed Bobby into a curtainless room with a scattering of cushions on the floor stunned her into silence.

Cute little wood animals and gnomes one found in markets? She'd eat the very words! Here was no punk's pastime, but artistic talent with a capital 'T'. It screamed out at her from every intricate frieze hanging on the walls, each one a landscape in wood. Awed, she moved closer to examine them. One depicted, in minutest detail, a steam-engine in an English country railway station; another steam-engine puffed proudly along the top of the Peruvian Andes; a third chuntered across an African landscape filled with antelopes, giraffes and elephants, that left her wondering where Bobby had learned such understanding of their magnificent bodies. What an eye he had! As brilliant as his magic hands. And then there were half a dozen street scenes, each filled with people, cars, tower blocks—all the *hoi polloi* of urban life meticulously etched and carved from mahogany, teak, pine, silver birch, the different woods adding colour and lustre.

'These are magnificent,' she gasped. 'Have you shown them to an art gallery?'

'I tried once, but the fellow wasn't interested.'

'Then he was a fool.'

'You're having me on?'

'I'm off duty all day,' she ignored his question, intent on her plan, 'and I'll come back with boxes and wadding for packing. I don't want to damage the carvings.'

'What are you going to do with them?'

'Show them to a friend of mine who has a gallery in Mayfair.'

'You're aiming high,' Bobby said, scratching his head.

'It's no more than you deserve. When I've finished with you, Bobby Millet, you'll be famous and rich enough to visit every single steam-engine in the world!'

Graham Koster, whose Bond Street gallery was the venue for young artists, was a friend of her godfather's, and greeted her warmly as one of his assistants helped Bobby carry the boxes into his office.

'Be completely frank with us,' she whispered to Graham as the carvings were ranged round the room. 'I don't want you giving us false hope.'

'That isn't my policy.' Carefully he examined the carvings while she and Bobby waited.

'I'm sorry Doc's wasting your time with these bits and pieces,' Bobby said after what seemed an hour but in reality was only a few moments. 'I'll repack 'em and go.'

'Not until we've discussed a contract,' Graham said.

'You mean you—you like my work?'

'More than like—I'm bowled over by it.'

Within weeks Bobby was in a studio of his own, subsidised by Graham, who assured them he was taking no risk.

He was proved right six months later when Bobby had his first show and sold every single piece, other than his best landscape which, red-faced and mumbling—the only time Tessa found him lost for words—he presented to her.

Then, with money in the bank, he went off to visit his beloved steam-engines, returning the following spring, ready to work again...

Tessa smiled reminiscently as she thought of the warm May dawn when, passing his studio on her way home after a long and exhausting emergency operation, she'd noticed his light on and gone to check he was well...

'Don't you ever sleep?' she asked when he opened the door, the wood shavings in his hair attesting to work rather than illness.

'Don't *you*?' he riposted.

Smiling, she entered his room. 'Working on anything new?'

'Yeah. I met a silversmith the day I came back from Peru,' he said, 'and we're having an exhibition together.'

'Graham doesn't like showing two artists at the same time.'

'He won't have a choice,' Bobby stated. 'The silver is sort of incorporated into the wood carvings.'

'Do you have a new piece to show me?' Tessa asked.

'Push, push!' he chided. 'Give us a few months...'

And she had. But it was August now, and time to pay him another call. With a day off in front of her, she went into the house to telephone him.

'Coming back for good?' he asked at once.

'Not yet.'

'I don't like it when my doc's ill.'

'I'm not ill,' she said at once, 'merely overworked. But I'm almost better, as you can see for yourself tomorrow, if you're free.'

'I'm always free for you. Come early and I'll treat you to lunch.'

At eleven next morning Tessa presented herself at Bobby's studio, disappointed to find the walls bare, though a few unfinished carvings on the large trestle-table by the window attested to his working.

'I was hoping you'd have something to show me,' she murmured, determinedly nonchalant because she knew he hated being pushed.

'I have,' he chuckled. 'But because of the silver and gold on them we keep them at the silver vaults. Jack— that's the guy I'm working with—has a stall there. We'll pop over there, and then have lunch.'

An hour later saw them wending their way through the conglomeration of stalls and little shops in the silver vaults—set beneath the London pavements in Chancery Lane, and famed for its antique silver.

Jack turned out to be a slightly older edition of Bobby without the punk hairdo, though the silver he sold was antique and ultra-conservative.

'It's what the tourists like,' he explained to Tessa, 'but my personal work is nothing like this.'

'Show her,' Bobby ordered, urging Tessa round the back of the stall, where Jack surreptitiously uncovered the pieces he and Bobby were preparing for their exhibition.

Tessa was mesmerised by their originality and beauty. Bobby's magnificently carved jungle landscapes gleamed with cunningly inset slivers of gold and silver. They glinted on the wooden trunks of trees, the wing of a flying bird, the muzzle of an animal. In a seascape, sailing-boats sparkled with a delicate tracery of golden rigging, and a full blown schooner, so alive it looked ready to sail off, glided upon billowing silver waves.

'Has Graham seen these?' Tessa asked.

'Yesterday,' Bobby replied. 'He's already set a date for the exhibition.'

Delightedly, Tessa straighted, then hurriedly bent down again.

'You ill?' Bobby asked.

'No.' She bent lower.

'Yes, you are. You're white as a ghost.' Bobby put his arm around Tessa in concern.

'You're imagining it.'

But he wasn't; nor had *she* imagined Patrick and Ingrid two stalls away from them! How awful it would be if he came over to her, and Bobby gave away her identity! There wasn't even time to tell Bobby about her charade!

Surreptitiously she rose a fraction and glanced over her shoulder, breathing a sigh of relief as she saw Patrick and Ingrid move off in the opposite direction.

'What the hell's wrong?' Bobby asked. 'You're shaking.'

'From hunger,' she fibbed, regretting the lie when Bobby insisted on taking her to a nearby Italian restaurant and stuffing her full of pasta.

Only as they were sipping their espresso did she come clean as to the real reason for her pallor, and Bobby laughed till he cried.

'You, a teenager in a miniskirt?' he said when he could finally speak. 'I don't believe it.'

'It suits me,' she informed him airily.

'I bet you look sensational,' he agreed, 'but not like my doc.'

'You make me sound awfully stuffy,' she protested, and he started laughing again.

'This Patrick of yours will blow his top when he finds out the truth. When are you going to tell him?'

'Soon. I'm not sure exactly when.'

'You haven't fallen for him, have you?'

'What a silly question.'

'I'm waiting for a silly answer.'

'Of course I haven't,' she said. 'He's brilliant at his work——'

'Like you.'

'And he can't stand career women.'

'Like you!'

'Exactly,' Tessa said.

'Then come clean with him and return to London. Jokes have a nasty habit of backfiring.' Bobby pulled a face. 'Fancy *me* telling you what to do! It doesn't seem right.'

'You're no longer my patient, Bobby, you're a friend, and I'll always welcome your opinion.'

As she drove away from London, Tessa thought over everything he had said. He was right, of course. She was becoming too involved with Patrick and it could lead nowhere she was willing to go.

She was despondently ruminating on this when she entered the kitchen and found Mrs Benson pounding at a mound of dough.

'Late-night baking?' Tessa asked, smiling with an effort.

The housekeeper grunted, her usual smile missing, and Tessa knew instantly that something was wrong.

'It's the Georgian bowl,' the woman said with the briefest of urging. 'The one Mr Anderson inherited from his great-grandmother. I went to clean it this morning and it's missing.'

'You must have mislaid it,' Tessa consoled.

'No, I haven't. It's always kept in a special place in the silver cupboard. Right at the back, behind a vase. But when I went to bring it out, it wasn't there.'

Tessa instantly remembered the night of Patrick's business dinner, and the open kitchen door through which Henry had escaped that evening. Dear lord! It was her fault for not locking the house properly. Heaven knew what else was gone! Shaking, she collapsed on to a chair.

'It's my fault, Mrs Benson, not yours,' she whispered, and went on to explain why.

Relieved that she wasn't to blame for the missing bowl, Mrs Benson did her best to comfort Tessa. But nothing she said overcame Tessa's guilt. Indeed, the more Tessa thought over what had happened, the worse she felt. It was because of this nonsensical charade, and her toing and froing between Greentrees and the Hall.

'I'd better ring the police,' she said.

'I've already done that. As soon as I couldn't find the bowl,' Mrs Benson said.

'What did you tell them?'

'That we'd been burgled. But I was in such a state I—I——' She shook her head. 'It was a good thing Mr Harper arrived when he did.'

'What's Mr Harper got to do with it?' Tessa asked sharply.

'He and Miss Mortensen saw the police car turn in here as they were leaving the Hall this morning for London, and he came in to find out what was wrong. As I said, I don't know what I'd have done without him—I was so upset that the police couldn't make head or tail of what I was saying. But Mr Harper took me round the house and the only thing missing was that bowl. And it's worth a fortune!'

'Don't remind me!' Tessa muttered. 'I'd better ring Uncle Martin and tell him. It's early morning in New Zealand, and I may catch him before he goes out.'

Tessa had never been more grateful for the miracle of the telephone than she was when, within ten seconds of dialling, she heard her godfather's voice twelve thousand miles away and learned that the Georgian bowl, far from being stolen, was with a jeweller in Iverton, who was mending its handle.

'I didn't think to mention it to Mrs Benson,' he concluded. 'Please tell her how sorry I am.'

Tessa did, the moment the call was over, and then rang the police to explain the bowl was safe.

'I think we should tell Mr Harper too,' Mrs Benson suggested, and Tessa, reluctant to go to see him, telephoned instead.

'He went to London with Miss Mortensen,' Withers informed her, 'and I'm not expecting them till tomorrow.'

So he and Ingrid were spending the night in London! In one bed, no doubt—it was hard to imagine Ingrid's missing such an opportunity.

Rubbish! her inner voice argued. I thought you'd decided Patrick wasn't the sort to mix business with pleasure.

He isn't, said Tessa's logical mind.

Oh, yeah? came the nasty little voice again. What free, red-blooded male could resist a beautiful woman who sets out to entice him?

So what if he didn't resist? After all, he was a free agent and could do as he liked with whom he liked! It was only the fact that he might be doing it with Ingrid that was infuriating! She wouldn't have cared a jot if it were with another girl.

At least, that was what Tessa told herself as she firmly refused to let other thoughts surface.

CHAPTER NINE

TESSA was halfway through her morning's work at the Hall, helping Withers go through the china-room, when she heard the throaty purr of Patrick's sports car.

It was an effort to restrain herself from rushing out to him. What a surprise he'd have if she did. Yet it wasn't because she wanted to see *him*, merely to let him know the bowl wasn't missing. Considering his kindness to Mrs Benson yesterday, the least she could do was assure him there were no burglars currently in the district!

She was at the door of the china-room when he strode in, handsomer than ever in a pale grey formal suit.

'I want to talk to you, Tessa,' he bit out.

'Same here,' she said eagerly.

'Come to my study in ten minutes.'

Not giving her a chance to reply, he turned on his heel and went out, his face set in such uncompromising lines that she was positive he had seen her at the silver vaults. As she thought of Bobby's dyed hair and earring, her mouth twitched with humour. Did Patrick honestly expect work-shy little Tessa to hang out with pin-striped City gents with rolled umbrellas?

'You'd better not keep Mr Harper waiting,' Withers cautioned her. 'The china will be here when you come back!'

Nodding, Tessa set off for the west wing, her good humour vanishing as she saw Ingrid in the main hall, as satisfied as a cat that had swallowed the canary! Where was the girl's subtlety? Or didn't she care if everyone knew she had spent the night in Patrick's bed?

'Where do you think *you're* going?' Ingrid demanded, suddenly appearing in front of her.

'To the big white chief!'

'How often do I have to warn you not to bother him? If there's anything you wish to know about anything, ask *me*.'

'I always do,' Tessa said without inflection. 'But he ordered me to go to him.'

Ingrid's lips tightened. 'In future I'll make sure he lets *me* deal with you.'

'Have you ever thought he might enjoy talking to the staff?' Tessa couldn't resist saying. 'Mr Harper might find it just the thing to relax him!'

Ingrid's laugh was scathing. 'Talking to you is hardly relaxing. I'd describe it as stupefying.'

Speechless, Tessa awarded this round to the Swedish girl, and felt a most unladylike urge to take a swipe at the lovely face in front of her. 'Do you have to be rude?' she asked.

'Coming from you, that's quite a question! But actually I was merely stating the obvious. Patrick has to keep his mind free for his work, not clutter it with domestic trivia and inane chatter. Why, only last night he conceived a sensational way of increasing the information on a disk.'

Tessa nearly asked, 'What time last night?' But though she bit back the question her expression gave her away, and the smile that curled Ingrid's mouth was answer enough.

'Far be it from me to come between a genius and his creativity,' Tessa managed to say, 'but I wouldn't boast about it if a boyfriend of mine concentrated on work when he was with me!'

'That's where we differ, my dear. Mr Harper and I are on the same intellectual level, and his knowing I understand his work is one of the things that makes us close. Beautiful girls are easy to come by when you've as much to offer as *he* has, but to find one with brains as well——'

'Oh, boy, do you love yourself!' Tessa laughed, and walked away. In the face of such conceit there was nothing else to do. Yet she had to concede the girl wasn't conceited so much as realistic. She was a stunner, and clever with it. And what was worse, she was clever in Patrick's field. Though he was adamant in his dislike of career women, he'd probably feel quite differently if the woman's career centred around himself!

Arriving at the study, she drew a deep breath and knocked on the door.

'What were you doing in the vaults yesterday?' he demanded the instant she entered.

So he *had* seen her. 'I was shopping.'

'For a silver dinner service?' he enquired sarcastically. 'I'd have thought a street market more your scene.'

'Shows how little you know me,' she said perkily.

'Enough to know you stole Mr Anderson's bowl!'

'What?' Tessa stared at him in horror. He might regard her as a scatter-brained low-brow, but did he really think her a thief? True, she had done her best to make him think her feckless, but had never given him cause to doubt her honesty.

'Well,' he grated, 'aren't you going to defend yourself?'

'I've nothing to defend,' she snapped. 'As it happens, Mr Anderson's bowl was——'

'Were you or were you not selling it to that yellow-haired punk you were making eyes at yesterday?'

'I wasn't making eyes at him!'

'You were practically in his arms behind the stall! And don't bother denying it, because I was only ten yards away from you!'

Realising he had seen Bobby put his arm around her when she had turned pale, she understood his misinterpretation of the gesture. But she was none the less furious that he considered her a thief.

'I'm waiting for an answer,' Patrick said harshly. 'What have you done with the Georgian bowl? There's no point lying to me. I know you took it, and I'll give you a chance to return it. I'll drive you to London myself if necessary, and wait while you collect it. I doubt if that pair behind the stall have sold it yet.'

Tessa listened to Patrick in astonishment. He believed her to be a thief, yet he was actually offering to help her retrieve the situation! Though it lessened her anger, she was unable to forgive his lack of faith in her character.

'If you're sure I stole the bowl, why haven't you told the police?'

Patrick shrugged. 'I've asked myself that since I saw you at the silver vaults yesterday. I guess I feel sorry for you.'

'Why?'

'You're intelligent and able, and you'll be wasting your life if you don't make proper use of it. Perhaps your attitude stems from your background.' He paused, brows drawn together in a frown. 'You're a mystery to me, Tessa, though it's clear you don't think beyond the moment, the instant gratification. Dammit, girl! You're eighteen and can make something of yourself, so don't spoil your future by being branded a thief. Return the bowl and hide it in a cupboard. I'm sure you can figure out a way for Mrs Benson to discover it herself.'

Tessa's anger evaporated completely. The poor darling was trying to blame her background for her dishonesty! Did he think she hailed from a thieves' den? Heavens, it was time she disclosed her identity. It was the very least she could do.

'There's something I have to tell you,' she said huskily. 'I'm not the person you think I am. I——'

'Sorry to intrude on you, Patrick,' Ingrid interrupted, coming in without knocking. 'But Mike has a problem to talk over with you.'

Muttering beneath his breath, Patrick strode out, and Tessa waited for Ingrid to say something nasty.

'What have you done to upset him this time?' the Swedish girl asked, running true to form.

'If you're anxious to know, ask him.'

'If you're anxious to keep the job, you'll tell me!'

'I may not wish to stay.' Tessa gave Ingrid an insolent stare, irritated that the girl was so lovely in a severely tailored black linen suit. If *I* wore that, she thought, I'd look as if I were going to a funeral. I guess one needs to be tall to get away with such stark simplicity.

'If you have doubts about staying on,' Ingrid's voice was unexpectedly conciliatory, 'you'd be better off leaving. You won't have trouble finding another job. I'll be happy to give you a reference.'

'You're really keen to be rid of me, aren't you?' Tessa retorted. 'I suppose you're scared of me.'

'Scared of a little nothing? That's ridiculous.'

'Is it? I think you're worried in case Mr Harper fancies me.'

Tessa made the statement deliberately to rile, and was triumphant as Ingrid's pale skin warmed to red.

'If Mr Harper was interested in a stupid girl like you,' came the hissed reply, 'he wouldn't be the man I know.'

'Maybe you *don't* know him.'

'You think not? How naïve you are! What Mr Harper and I feel for one another is——' Ingrid stopped. 'But why am I wasting my energy talking to you? You're nothing in our lives, and it will be better if you go.'

'I'll only take that kind of order from the boss,' Tessa said, wondering exactly how deep a relationship Ingrid and Patrick had.

'What kind of order?' Patrick asked from the doorway.

Tessa swung round to him. 'Ingrid's suggesting I leave.'

'Why?' He spoke the question to Ingrid, who glided closer to him before replying.

'Because there isn't enough for her to do here. And it isn't good for young people to be bored.'

'That's quite true,' he said lightly. 'We'll have to find Tessa more to do.'

Ingrid went to speak, then thought better of it and shrugged.

Tessa, watching the two of them standing close, thought what an excellent foil they made for one another: both tall, slim, and elegant as greyhounds, Ingrid's silvery fairness accentuating Patrick's dark masculinity. A wave of pure rage engulfed her, obliterating thought and reason, and leaving her a quivering, insensate mass.

But as clarity returned, one question loomed large, obliterating everything else. Why did the sight of Patrick and Ingrid together disturb her so much? No longer could she run from the answer. It was jealousy, pure and simple. Except jealousy was neither pure nor simple, but distorting and illogical, making you do things you'd never do if you were sane.

And she certainly wasn't sane. How *could* she be if she thought, even for a moment, that she could be happy with a man like Patrick? Why, his very attitude to career women was the biggest turn-off! Yet if that were true, how come she ached for him?

Her surgeon's mind probed the question as delicately as her skilful hands would a patient. It was Sir Denis's fault. By forcing her to admit she didn't relish living the rest of her life alone, he had made her receptive to a man who was handsome, humorous and intelligent. Obstinate and bad-tempered too, she admitted, though this increased rather than detracted from his appeal, for who would be happy living with a paragon?

She became aware of Patrick's eyeing her, and, meeting his blue gaze, suddenly imagined him married to Ingrid. He was already half married, in fact, considering the way she organised everything he did. What a fool he was—all-seeing in his work, yet blind in his personal life!

Anger returned. A man who was so dumb deserved to be made a fool of, and as far as she was concerned it wasn't only Ingrid who was going to go on pulling the wool over his eyes. She'd do the same herself, and carry on with her charade.

'I'd like to talk to Tessa alone,' Patrick murmured, guiding Ingrid to the door, and he did not speak again until he had closed it. 'Well, I'm waiting.'

'For what?' Tessa asked.

'Before Ingrid interrupted us, you said there was something you wished to tell me.' His voice was steady, almost as if he was trying to reassure her that he wouldn't be angry, no matter what she said.

'I've forgotten what it was,' she replied.

'I don't believe you. Before Ingrid interrupted us, you were saying you weren't the person I thought you were, and I'd be obliged if you explained yourself.'

'Oh, that,' she shrugged. 'I meant I'm not a thief, and I didn't take the bowl.'

'Then why were you at the vaults?'

'I've already told you. To visit my friends. I'm very close to Bobby.' Well, that was no lie. As a surgeon she knew him intimately!

'Does he own the stall?' came the next question.

'No, it belongs to the other boy. Bobby took me there to meet him.'

'And to sell him the bowl?'

Tessa almost stamped her foot. 'I've told you I didn't take it! Why can't you believe me?'

Patrick bent towards her and caught her by the shoulders, his hands large upon the fragile bones. 'If only I could,' he muttered. 'But logic warns me not to.'

'Forget logic and trust your feelings.'

'They're too jumbled when I'm with you. And when you stare at me like that...'

'Like what?'

'You know very well what,' he groaned, and pulled her into his arms.

Even when she stood on tiptoe, the top of her head didn't reach his chin, and he swung her off her feet, cradling her without effort as their mouths met and merged, simultaneously parting for tongues to entwine.

As she succumbed to the heat and warmth of him, Tessa marvelled at her lack of inhibition. It was incredible that she, who considered herself emotionally reserved, should feel such abandonment at his touch, the taste of him, the smell of him.

Trembling, she nestled closer, curving her body into his. He murmured deep in his throat, and sank with her on to the nearby sofa. With his hands no longer holding her, they were free to roam her body, lightly skimming the delicate line of neck to rest upon the gentle swell of her breasts.

At the touch of his fingers a burning flame engulfed her. Her nipples hardened and her stomach was pierced with sweet shafts of desire that were echoed by the movements of his body.

'Patrick,' she whispered upon his mouth. 'Oh, Patrick——'

With a suddenness that shocked her, he pushed her away and stood up. 'This is madness,' he muttered, his face dark with anger as well as passion. 'Don't use your sex on me, Tessa; I won't be fooled that way!'

Tessa was lost for words. Did he think she had deliberately set out to entice him in order to make him believe in her innocence? My God, how low his opinion was of her!

'I nearly succeeded, didn't I?' she taunted. 'Another minute and you'd have been well and truly gone!'

'Don't kid yourself. I was simply interested in discovering how far *you* were prepared to go.'

'All the way,' she mocked, hands on hips. 'But not with a man as old as you! You should be ashamed of yourself, taking advantage of me!'

'I didn't hear you objecting.'

'I was experimenting.'

'So was I,' he replied. 'You're not my idea of a normal teenager.'

'Is that why you fancy me?'

He laughed. 'I don't. I've too much sense. Love-affairs are complicated enough without trying to make it with a girl from a different generation.'

'Then don't touch the goods if you're not going to buy!'

A dull flush rose in his face and Tessa knew she had hit his pride. But he came out fighting. 'Then don't *you* bat those soulful eyes at me!'

'I didn't realise how poor your resistance was. You aren't a boy, Mr Harper. Where's your control?'

This time the blow was too hard for him to fight back, and he gave a deep sigh. 'I'm sorry, Tessa. It won't happen again.'

'You said that once before. But I think you're a wolf, and I'll thank you not to prowl around me.' She was by

the door when he called her name, and she half turned.
'Yes?'

'Remember my advice about the bowl. Hide it away,
and then ensure Mrs Benson finds it.'

Not deigning to reply, Tessa went out, slamming the
door hard.

Though angered by his low opinion of her, she kept
remembering the way he had kissed her. No matter what
he said, and regardless of his relationship with Ingrid,
he was definitely attracted to her, which went to show
he wasn't the faithful type!

Or did he feel his affair with Ingrid didn't necessitate
it? Tessa's disgust with him grew. If she really was a
flighty young girl, she'd have met him halfway and enjoyed the moment—or hours! But she was Tessa Redfern,
a woman of circumspection, who was as likely to have
a casual affair as operate without surgical gloves! She
sighed heavily. She couldn't go against her nature any
more than Patrick Harper could go against *his*.

Which brought her back to square one, and the sad
but inescapable admission that they were two people
walking parallel lines. Einstein had been convinced that
at some point parallel lines met, but even *his* genius had
never been able to prove it.

When she returned home later that day, Mrs Benson
remarked on her miserable expression. 'I thought
working at the Hall was fun for you.'

'Not today it wasn't.'

'Did you tell Mr Harper we found the bowl?'

'I was on the verge of doing so when he accused *me*
of stealing it.'

'You're joking!'

'Unfortunately not.'

Hearing the full story—albeit a heavily censored
version—Mrs Benson was all for going to the Hall to

'put that Mr Harper of yours straight!', and Tessa had a hard job persuading her not to.

'I want Patrick to trust me of his own accord,' she explained.

'He would, if he knew you as you really are,' Mrs Benson said forthrightly. 'I do wish you'd put an end to this silly farce.'

'I won't carry it on much longer. I'll just give him a bit longer to think things over. Once he has, I'm hoping he'll realise I couldn't be a thief. So promise me you won't breathe a word to anyone.'

Mrs Benson sniffed. 'You know you can wind me round your little finger.'

Tessa nodded, wishing she could do the same with Patrick. What a hope! He wasn't the type to be ruled by passion—or love, come to that. He was content ploughing a lone furrow and taking his pleasures when it suited him.

Unless, of course, Ingrid caught him at a weak moment.

CHAPTER TEN

THE next morning, Tessa's anger at Patrick had slightly abated, and she was forced to admit he would be less suspicious of her if she looked more like her old self. Yet her old self had been dull, and seemed even duller by comparison with her present cheeky persona.

But the time was ripe for her to be a little truer to her real self. After all, had Patrick presented himself as a long-haired hippy she might well have misjudged his character too!

In this charitable mood, she contacted Mr Withers to ask if it was convenient to take off the whole day.

'We owe you a few days,' he informed her. 'If you'd care to have them now...'

'No, thanks, one day will be fine.'

Light-heartedly she set off for Iverton, agreeably surprised to find a highly modern hairdressing salon called 'Antoine'.

Antoine himself turned out to hail from Leeds, and was small and thin, with soulful eyes that grew more soulful as he regarded her unruly hair.

'I suppose you wish to have it set in the same style as this?' he asked dolefully.

'Unless you can think of a better way,' she said, bravely deciding that the worst he could do was cut it too short. 'I'm willing to leave the style to you.'

Her words acted on him like a shot of adrenalin, and the change in him was remarkable. Before her very eyes he appeared to grow in stature and confidence, and with murmured incantations, as if calling on some inner god for inspiration, he lifted a curl here, twisted a curl there, and then threw a voluminous pink cape round her shoulders.

'First we will wash it. Then I will decide what to do.'

A plump girl with a crew cut—which did little to inspire Tessa's confidence, and almost made her flee—gave her hair the most vigorous wash of its life before returning her to Antoine, who was waiting for her with scissors poised.

Crossing her fingers, Tessa sat down and closed her eyes, each snip of the blades sending her spirits plunging.

An hour later she stared into the mirror, bemused at the stranger staring back at her.

'You're a miracle worker, Antoine! I can't believe it's me!'

Twisting her head this way and that, she admired the sleek swirl of tamed red-gold hair that clung to her scalp, showing the lovely rounded curve of her head before it broke into a soft froth of curls that caressed her nape.

'You'll find it easy to keep,' Antoine assured her.

'You think so? Whenever it's set smooth, it always goes frizzy after a few days.'

'That's because of bad cutting. If *mine* goes frizzy on you, I'll reset it for free.'

In the face of such confidence, Tessa's own grew, and, feeling like a new woman, she wandered along the high street. Her reflection in a window reminded her she wasn't all new, and, thoroughly disliking her skimpy denim skirt and outsize tank-top, she set off in search of clothes more in keeping with the image she wished to project. Still young, of course, but old enough for Patrick to stop thinking of her as a child.

A blast of music told her she was nearing the shop where she had bought her present outfit, and, head lowered, she slunk past it, delighted to spy a smart boutique on the other side of the road.

It was odd that she hadn't noticed it before. But then she hadn't noticed Antoine's salon either, though he had been in Iverton three years. But whenever she stayed with Uncle Martin, she was so pleased to relax that she gave little thought to her appearance.

When her car finally drew up in the small, curving drive of the Queen Anne house the back was laden with parcels, and Mrs Benson made no attempt to hide her astonishment and delight at Tessa's appearance.

'I'm glad you're finally taking an interest in yourself.'

'Don't I always—apart from the last few weeks, I mean?'

'Let's say you're always neat and tidy, but now you're a real picture.'

'Don't go overboard,' Tessa chuckled.

'I'm not. I mean every word.' Mrs Benson walked round her, lightly touching the shining red-gold curls. 'Bought new clothes too, have you?'

For answer, Tessa opened one of the packages, disclosing a mint-green cotton dress with a finely tucked bodice and nipped-in waist.

'Do you think Patrick will approve?' Taking it out, she held it against herself.

'You aren't planning to wear it for work?' the housekeeper exclaimed.

'Too true.'

'Fancy him, do you?'

Tessa hesitated. She knew the question was prompted by love, and decided it was mean to lie. 'Yes, I do. But he loathes career women, and I don't stand a chance with him.'

'Then why the finery?'

'I'd like him to see me as I really am. I suppose you could call it vanity.'

'I prefer to call it being hopeful! Men often say one thing and then do another—especially when they fall in love.'

'Patrick doesn't believe in love—or marriage.'

'Neither did my husband, rest his soul!'

Tessa laughed and hugged Mrs Benson tightly before carrying her parcels upstairs.

The next morning, in her new green dress, she set off for the Hall. She couldn't wait to see Patrick's face when he set eyes on her, and she fantasised about his reaction. How fabulous it would be if he fell in love with her on sight!

Chiding herself for being stupidly romantic—and she a logical, hard-headed surgeon too—she almost ran the last few yards, and breathlessly pushed open the heavy oak door.

Luck was on her side, for the very man she wanted was emerging from the sitting-room. Her heart raced. She hadn't seen him for a day, and the sheer handsomeness of him hit her. Tall, slimly built, but whipcord strong, he emanated such sexuality that her body tingled. Motionless, she waited for him to come closer, but with nary a glance in her direction he walked past her, his expression intent, his eyes glazed.

Indignantly she stared after him. What a let-down!

Mr and Mrs Withers' appreciation of her changed appearance, and Emmy's and Eva's 'ooh's and 'aah's, did much to re-establish her self-esteem, though it wasn't until she was setting out the morning coffee in the sitting-room, and Mike gave a wolf-whistle and asked if she had won the Irish Sweepstake, that Tessa suddenly wondered if Patrick would think her new appearance and wardrobe came from her ill-gotten gains in selling the silver bowl.

If only she'd thought of that before! But it was too late to revert to her old image, and if he *did* eventually notice it and pass a sarcastic comment she hoped she'd find the right response.

'I've nothing else to spend my wages on,' she answered Mike.

'I'm in the same boat. Living here is lousy for my social life, but great for my bank balance. Fancy helping me decrease it by having dinner with me tonight?'

'I'm not sure Mr Harper would approve,' she hedged.

'I'm not inviting Patrick—only you!'

'Not inviting me where?' The man himself materialised directly beside them.

'I'm trying to persuade Tessa to have dinner with me,' Mike answered. 'Doesn't she look great?'

Patrick studied her as if she were a butterfly impaled by a pin. But his expression was unreadable as he turned to the younger man.

'If you can spare a moment, we should discuss that new program you're doing.'

The two of them drifted away, and Tessa continued pouring the coffee, then waited quietly in the corner until the cups were returned to the trolley and she was free to wheel it out.

She was on the threshold when Patrick strode after her.

'Any more coffee left?'

Luckily there was, and she poured him a cup.

'It's cold.' Irritated, he plonked it back on the trolley. 'Why isn't the coffee served from an electric percolator?'

'Ask Ingrid,' Tessa said sweetly. '*She* gives the orders.'

'Surely not for such a simple thing?'

'She issues orders for *everything*.'

Patrick peered at the plate of biscuits. 'Not very exciting,' he observed. 'All the cream cakes gone, I suppose?'

'Chance would be a fine thing.'

'I beg your pardon?'

'There weren't any to begin with. We're only allowed to serve plain biscuits.'

'You're joking!'

'Ingrid wasn't. It was her order. She says cream cakes require forks and napkins and would take longer to eat.'

Patrick said nothing, and Tessa was sorry she couldn't think of any other carping comments to make about the Swedish girl.

'You could do worse than date Mike,' Patrick said unexpectedly. 'He's the right age for you.'

'You think so?' she seethed.

'Definitely. He fancied you the minute you came to work here, and he's a steady chap.'

'You mean he doesn't have a roving eye like you?'

'I'm not interested in marriage,' Patrick said loftily, 'so I'm entitled to rove.'

'Thanks for your advice regarding Mike,' she managed to say through clenched teeth. 'I may accept it.'

So much for her new image! Why bother when it attracted the wrong man? Patrick hadn't even noticed it, let alone commented on it. As far as *he* was concerned, she was the same girl he had first met examining the hole in the wall!

Tessa was fuming as she helped with lunch. As soon as it was over, she'd dash home and change back to her 'sloppy Joe' image.

But Mrs Withers put paid to this by asking Tessa to sort through the attics. 'I took a peep at them over the weekend, and from the mess they're in they haven't been cleaned or sorted out for years.'

Tessa glanced ruefully at her pristine dress, and Mrs Withers winked and handed her a voluminous apron.

'Start on the biggest one first,' she ordered, 'and take plenty of dusters and a torch.'

'Don't tell me there's no electricity there!'

'There is,' Mrs Withers beamed, 'but the smallest attic is more than twenty feet square, and they're only lit by central bulbs.'

Donning the overall, and collecting a mound of dusters, Tessa mounted the stairs. It was the first time she was able to roam the house freely, and she found it larger than she remembered and in surprisingly good order.

The first-floor bedrooms were occupied by members of the think-tank, and the floor above by the live-in staff, which still left many bedrooms empty. But perhaps Patrick intended to expand. From what she read in the City news, there was no limit to how big his company could grow, for his ideas were way ahead of his competitors'.

But enough of Patrick! She had better things to think about! Reaching the third floor, she paused to catch her breath. The atmosphere here was different, clean and dry, but with an unlived-in air, as though no footsteps had walked the long, dim corridors for years.

Quietly she opened a few doors. Antiquated bathrooms and more staff bedrooms stuffed with Victorian furniture that would fetch a good price at auction, she mused. Her interest quickening, she stepped forward to examine a heavily carved dressing-table, then abruptly drew back. There was a job to do first, and she dared not give in to her collector's curiosity until it was completed.

The thought lent wings to her feet, and she almost ran up the last flight of stairs that brought her under the eaves. It was certainly dim here, and Tessa switched on the light and proceeded along a linoleum-covered passageway, with attics either side of her. There were six in all, and she peeped into each one. They were so chock-a-block with boxes and trunks, to say nothing of broken toys, umbrella stands and other junk, that she knew it would be impossible to get rid of the rubbish by herself. It required an army of cleaners and a removal van!

Resolutely she entered the largest attic.

Mrs Withers had said no one had entered it for years, but Tessa decided centuries was more like it! Excitement trembled inside her, born of a hunter's instinct that told her she was going to unearth something momentous.

The last occasion she had felt this, she had discovered an eighteenth-century chamber-pot, a less-than ro- mantic find which now housed an aspidistra on her kitchen window-ledge. But there were sure to be more inspiring finds here, and she turned on the light and slowly swivelled round.

There were cobwebs everywhere, and with flailing arms she brushed them to the floor, almost tripping over a mound of old curtains in the process. Weavings and fabrics were her weakness, and she bent to examine them, disappointed to find they were moth-eaten and falling to pieces.

Dust rose in a cloud around her, stinging her throat and her eyes, and she searched for a window. There was a narrow one at the far side, which meant climbing over numerous cartons to reach it, and she abandoned the idea in favour of examining the boxes nearest to her.

Bending, she lifted a lid. Ugh! A dank smell of mould filled her nostrils, and, regretting her lack of rubber gloves, she gingerly prodded at various mildewed Victorian suits and dresses before hurriedly closing the lid. Box number one for the bonfire!

An hour later, her eyelashes and bright hair covered with dust, there were four more boxes ready for dis- posal. That left an ancient tin trunk and three tea-chests to be examined, and she sat back on her heels for a breather.

Who had been the last person to examine these rooms? Thinking of the case of musty, unworn baby clothes which now stood by the door, ready to go, it was painfully easy to visualise a young mother crying for the child who had never worn them. Had it been Lord Finworth's great-great-grandmother, or aunt five times removed? How wonderful to trace one's lineage back hundreds of years, to know that the blood flowing in *your* veins had flowed in the veins of an Elizabethan lady or a courtier to King Charles.

Yet what difference did it make who your ancestors were? Bobby had no idea who his father was, yet he was bursting with talent, and that was what counted.

Rising, she flicked on her torch and set to work again. The trunk was locked, and the tea-chests were too securely nailed for her to open, and she ran down to the kitchen in search of a hammer and screwdriver.

Pedro, busy making tea, burst out laughing at the sight of her. 'Been taking a dust bath?'

'Almost. Care to help me open a few tea-chests?'

'I only drink coffee!'

Pulling a face at him, she hurried away. Because she was concerned not to injure her hands, it took her a while to prise off the first lid, and as she lifted it a sigh of disappointment escaped her. More rotting fabric. One of the Finworth ancestors had obviously been a compulsive buyer of material!

Resignedly, she drew out a rolled piece of brocade, holding it away from her in case it fell to pieces. But it was dry and firm to the touch, and heavy too, as if it was wrapped round something.

Puzzled, she undid it and found herself holding a narrow roll of canvas. She carefully uncurled it and stared at a two-foot-square painting, afraid to believe what her senses were telling her.

Forcing down her rising tension, she scanned every inch of it, noting the masterly composition of the figures, the delicacy of the brush strokes, the serene style. She was no expert, but it was impossible to live with Uncle Martin and not imbibe a little of his knowledge, and she was almost certain she was holding a Titian! It was an incredible thought, and she drew a deep breath to steady herself. But her hands were trembling as she continued examining the rest of the contents.

An hour later, the three tea-chests sorted through, fifteen paintings lay at her feet. None would fetch less than a hundred thousand pounds, and three—unless she was very much mistaken—were old masters: a Poussin, a Tintoretto, and a Raphael any museum would give ten years of its budget for!

Her first instinct was to rush to Patrick—not that he deserved to be shown such a windfall after his horrid behaviour to her! Visualising his disbelief, his wonderment, she felt an urge to show off her discoveries in the most exciting manner possible, and decided to set them out in one of the unoccupied rooms on the floor below.

Surreptitiously she carried the canvases into the largest bedroom and spread them on the floor in front of the four-poster bed. If such magnificence had been left in the tea-chests, heaven knew what treasure the trunk housed!

Locking the bedroom and pocketing the key, she raced back to the attic. The lock on the trunk was large and rusty, but nothing was going to deter her, and a firm blow with the hammer soon rendered it useless. With a deep breath, she lifted the lid.

What a disappointment! It was chock-a-block with musty family documents and household accounts. True, many dated back to the sixteenth century and were probably of great interest to archivists, but their financial value was minor compared with the paintings.

Disappointed, she sat back on her heels. Her foot knocked against the torch and it slid along the floor. As

she reached to retrieve it, her face was inches away from
the right-hand wall, and she found herself staring at a
two-foot-high door, skilfully papered over to match the
rest of the peeling paper on the wall around it.

There was no visible handle and, adrenalin flowing,
she carefully pressed round the edges. She was on the
verge of giving up when there was a faint click beneath
her fingers, and the door creaked back to reveal an inner
darkness.

Corpses! she thought wildly. Skeletons and skulls. Re-
minding herself that she was a surgeon and used to
bodies, she flicked on the torch. The beam shone on an
eight-foot-square cavity no more than four feet high, in
which stood an enormous wooden linen-chest. A bride's
trousseau, or more fabric!

Crawling in, she shone the torch on the floor to make
sure there were no spiders, and sat down. She hadn't
enjoyed herself so much in years. It was as if she were
a child again, in a world of astonishing and untold
wonders. But if she didn't hurry the spell would be
broken by anxious grown-ups coming to see what she
was doing!

Lifting the lid, she saw yellowing paper parcels of
various shapes and sizes. Weighing one in her hand, she
tried to guess its contents. A gold or silver object? No,
probably china from the weight of it.

She was right too, for, peeling away the paper, she saw
a little vase, no more than six inches high. Its colours
were glowingly luminous, almost as though it was lit from
within. But it was Tessa who was alight, for she was
positive she was holding a priceless Ming.

Reverently she placed it on the floor and gingerly un-
wrapped the rest of the contents. An hour later, two
dozen little vases and three large bowls from the same
period stood in front of her.

If she found nothing else, these objects alone would give Patrick enough money to buy into Allinson Software, or to buy the company entirely!

She must break the news to him at once. Bending double, she crawled out of the secret room, but as she straightened an ominous thought struck her.

What if she were wrong, and the paintings and china were nothing other than brilliant copies? After all, who was crazy enough to leave such untold wealth mouldering in an attic for years? Lord Finworth had been noted for his eccentricity, but to have done this was plain dotty!

But, dotty or not, the possibility existed that her discoveries weren't genuine. She frowned. The last thing she fancied was to make a fool of herself in Patrick's eyes. Far better to ascertain if her judgement was correct.

And she knew exactly the man to tell her: Angus Boswell. A retired director of a prestigious auction house, he now ran a little antique shop in Iverton as a hobby, leaving it once a month to dine with Uncle Martin. Tessa had known him for years, and would take his word as to whether she had uncovered trash or treasure.

If treasure, she would put everything in the bedroom and show it to Patrick in one fell swoop. Assuming it was possible to get him into the bedroom! Bearing in mind his present attitude towards her, it was the last place he'd elect to be with her.

She was rewrapping the china when she heard footsteps. Heart racing, she crawled out of the secret room and closed the door. Don't let it be Patrick, she prayed. After her wonderful plan to surprise him, it would be a shame if it fell flat.

But it was Mike's blond head that appeared through the gloom. 'Hi,' he greeted her. 'I heard you were here. Require help?'

'Aren't you working?'

'You're worse than Ingrid! I'm taking a break and visiting a beautiful lady in an attic.'

'You make it sound very romantic,' Tessa said, regretting her comment as Mike moved closer.

'I can put it into action,' he murmured.

'No, thanks.'

'Why not?' He drew her close and feathered little kisses from her forehead to her mouth.

Tessa's instinctive reaction was to push him away, but she resisted it. Why not let him kiss her? He was an eligible man, and a nice one—the sort who wouldn't object to a wife with a career of her own. But, though his lips were soft and his kiss was expert, she felt nothing, and gently wriggled free of him.

'I think I've rushed you,' he said.

Forbearing to say he'd have no more success if he went as slowly as a tortoise, she made a play of closing the lid of the box nearest to her.

'Sure I can't be of help?' he repeated.

'No, thanks.'

'You didn't object to my kissing you, did you?'

'No.'

'What if I did it again?'

'No to that, too.'

His reply was drowned by the sound of other footsteps, and he stepped back from Tessa as Patrick loomed in the doorway.

'I hope I'm not disturbing you both?' he asked with heavy sarcasm.

'Not in the least.' Mike was not to be fazed. 'I was just going.'

He sauntered off, but Patrick remained where he was, his expression nasty. 'Hiding here to avoid work?'

'Clever of you to guess!' she snapped.

For the first time he noticed the dust and cobwebs covering her. 'Why are you nosing around here?'

'Seeing if there's anything worth pinching!'

He looked ready to explode, and she relented. 'Mrs Withers asked me to sort through this rubbish.'

'Oh.' He simmered down, though was still scowling. 'There's certainly enough of it. I'll call in a junk man to clear it out.'

'Without looking at it? You may be throwing away something valuable.'

'Not if the rest of the house is anything to go by. Apart from a few antique pieces, my great-uncle cherished the worst of Victoriana. Anyway, you've sorted through things long enough. It's gone five and you are to go home.'

Realising she had to obey him, which meant tearing up four flights again when he was out of sight, she signalled him to lead the way, afraid that if she went first he'd notice the hidden door.

'Dining with Mike tonight?' he enquired as they walked along the passage.

'Trying to push me off on another man?'

'You could do worse.'

'Worse than you?'

'Don't be rude. You'd better watch your tongue in your next job! Other employers won't be as easygoing with you as I am!'

'They won't try to seduce me either!'

He choked off a reply, then muttered, 'How often do I have to apologise? I've already said it won't happen again.'

Tessa slowed her steps. 'Maybe I want it to.'

He stopped completely. 'That's a very sudden change of heart.'

'It's a woman's prerogative.'

'But you're a teenager!'

'You fancy me, though, don't you?'

For answer, he scanned her from top to toe, and she was chagrined that he had chosen the least propitious moment to do so. Enveloped in Mrs Withers' voluminous apron, she resembled a parcel with legs, while her hair resembled a bird's nest!

'I'm not at my best right now,' she mumbled.

'You don't say?' His smile was mean. 'The dank smell you're emanating would be a great deterrent for any female who has to go out alone at night, and that apron of yours protects your virginity better than a chastity belt!'

'How do you know I'm a virgin?' The question popped out of its own volition, and Tessa longed to kick herself. Especially when she couldn't interpret the strange expression that crossed Patrick's face.

'Old-fashioned of me to imagine you were,' he drawled, and, before she could think of a suitable answer, he turned on his heel and strode away.

The instant he was out of sight, she raced back to the attic and stealthily carried the china to the bedroom beneath. Then, locking the door, she raced off to call Angus Boswell.

Afraid of being overheard, she took a chance and went into the sitting-room, breathing a sigh of relief to find it empty. With trembling fingers she punched out his number, relieved when he answered at the first ring.

'It's Tessa,' she whispered. 'Sorry it's short notice, but I'd like to show you a few things urgently.'

'How urgently?'

'Now! I can be with you in half an hour.'

'I'll wait for you.'

Tiptoeing into the butler's pantry where Withers kept a canvas holdall, she furtively carried the bag upstairs and filled it with a small selection of the Ming china, and the three old masters. Then, making certain the coast was clear, she tiptoed downstairs and out of the house.

CHAPTER ELEVEN

THE canvas holdall was heavy, and Tessa was breathing fast when she finally put it into her car and set off for Iverton and Angus Boswell.

His antique shop was off the high street, and as she parked in front of it—no meters here, thank goodness—he came out to see if she required a helping hand. He was a courtly man in his late sixties, with sparse grey hair and sharp grey eyes.

Gratefully she gave him the holdall, and he raised an eyebrow at its weight. 'Found a cache of old Roman coins?' he joked.

'Far more valuable than that—I hope.'

'You're whetting my curiosity.'

Tessa followed him into the shop and through to his private office. He set the holdall on his desk and waited for her to unzip it. She did so with shaking hands, as nervous as if she were performing her first operation. Her fingers were all thumbs and the zip stuck halfway, defying all effort to move it until Angus gently pushed her aside and did it himself.

'They're paintings and china,' she explained, her throat so dry it was difficult to speak. 'I found them in an attic in Lord Finworth's house. I—er—I'm a friend of Patrick Harper, his great-nephew. He was the sole heir.'

Without another word she lifted out the topmost roll of canvas and handed it to Angus. Carefully he unwound it, then without comment began lifting out the entire contents. Neither by word, gesture nor expression did he give away his thoughts as he painstakingly examined each item.

The minutes ticked by. Twenty, forty, an hour. Dog-eared books were riffled through, records studied, a long call made to a curator in Paris, and a longer one to another in Munich, and all the time Tessa remained motionless, her heart pounding like a piston.

After what seemed an eternity, Angus turned to her, voice low, colour high. 'The paintings are genuine—there's no doubt whatsoever—and come from the Baron Wimburg Collection. They were sold to an unknown private buyer, reputed to be English, more than a hundred years ago. The value of them in today's market is almost impossible to assess. Certainly a king's ransom.'

Tessa's breath came out on a tremulous sigh. 'I thought so but . . . I was afraid to believe it. A king's ransom, eh?'

'Without counting the china! I'm pretty sure all the pieces are Ming, but I won't swear to it. I'm dining with a friend tonight who's an expert in this field, and I'd like to have his opinion on them.'

'That's fine with me. Will you call as soon as you've any news?'

Promising he would, Angus escorted her to her car.

Tessa drove back to Greentrees in a delirium of excitement. Mrs Benson had left for a church meeting, leaving a casserole in the microwave, but Tessa didn't have the patience to sit still and eat. She quickly changed her dusty clothes and paced the floor as she deliberated what to do.

Was it better to wait until Angus called her, or should she contact Patrick now and let him know him the fabulous news about the paintings?

She was still undecided when a car screeched to a stop in the drive, and, peering through the window, she was astonished to see the very man she was thinking of. She ran to open the front door and he barged straight in, white around the mouth, eyes glittering.

'I've caught you this time,' he hissed, gripping her arm and dragging her into the sitting-room.

'Caught me where?' she gasped, trying to pull free.

'Don't play the innocent! I saw you sneaking from my house with that hold-all and——'

'I wasn't sneaking!' she flared.

'You damn well were! That's why I followed you.'

'You followed me?'

'Right to the antique shop. What the hell did you find in the attic that made you rush off to that man?'

'I—I——' She was furious with Patrick for mis-judging her again, and tears of rage spilled down her cheeks. Was he too blind to know she cared for his best interests? He really was an ungrateful swine!

'Quit snivelling, you won't get round me that way,' he rasped, dragging her towards the door.

'Where are you taking me?'

'To Iverton. I intend finding out what that man bought from you.'

'He isn't there,' she cried. 'He'll have gone home by now.'

'Then we'll look for his address in the phone book. Dammit, Tessa, I gave you a chance to redeem yourself, and what the hell do you do? Repay me by stealing some of *my* things!'

Boiling with indignation, Tessa rounded on him in fury, but her retort was drowned by the ringing of the telephone. Reaching for it, she heard Angus at the other end.

'An emperor's ransom this time!' he said jubilantly. 'Each piece is perfect, and some are so rare they've never appeared on the market.'

'That's wonderful news, Angus,' she murmured. 'But I'd like you to tell Mr Harper yourself. He's right beside me.'

She handed the receiver to Patrick, and, watching him as he listened to Angus, she wondered how he must feel to know that even if he sold only a fraction of the Ming and one of the paintings he would have sufficient money to fulfil all his ambitions.

'Tessa, what can I say?'

With a start, she saw he had replaced the receiver and was standing in front of her.

'What can I say,' he repeated huskily, 'other than to apologise and grovel at your feet?'

'It isn't necessary to grovel,' she said coldly. 'I just hope this has taught you to give people the benefit of the doubt and not jump to nasty conclusions about them.'

'Generally I don't.'

'You always think the worst of *me*.'

'I know. And I can't fathom out why.' He shook his head in bewilderment. 'You annoy me so much that I—I guess I lose my temper with you.'

Her spirits sank and she turned away.

'I suppose it's because I dislike the idea of your wasting your life,' he added. 'I dislike waste in any form.'

As she felt the same, her anger lessened. 'You can't regiment the human race, you know.'

'Agreed. But at the moment we're discussing *your* potential. I'm convinced you can do much more with your life, Tessa.'

Spirits rising, she made herself pout. 'You're always saying that. It will serve you right if I take your advice and end up a hard-bitten tycoon!'

'Heaven forbid,' he groaned. 'I'm simply suggesting you train for a worthwhile job until you meet the right man.'

Tessa hung on to her temper. 'There you go again, talking like someone out of the ark! If I had a "worthwhile" job, as you call it, I wouldn't want to pack it in when I married. You know something? It would serve you right if you fell madly in love with a highly successful career woman! Oh, boy, what a laugh that would be!'

'I'd prefer to be a bachelor forever,' he said loftily.

'Don't tell me you *might* actually marry one day?'

'I have every intention of doing so.' He half leaned against the side of the settee, arms folded across his chest, rangy frame relaxed. 'It's pretty pointless building up an empire and having no sons to leave it to.'

'What will you do if you only have daughters?' she couldn't resist asking. 'It would serve you right if you sired a whole brood of career women!'

'That's enough to put me off marriage completely.'

'Good. Then I've done my good deed for the day,' she said with the cheek of the young girl she was supposed to be. 'I'll have saved some poor female from the clutches of a chauvinist.'

He chuckled. 'You and your sharp tongue! Be careful you don't cut yourself with it.'

'I'll more likely cut *you*.'

'Is that so?' he said, straightening and pulling her in one fell swoop close against his chest. 'Let's see you try.'

But he gave her no chance, for his lips fastened on hers, making it impossible for her to do anything other than stand there like a statue or respond. But the warmth of his lips, their softness, their gentle pressure, made it inevitable that she return the passion swiftly growing in him, a passion that increased as her mouth parted beneath his and he found her tongue to be not sharp, as he had said, but sweet and soft, its warm moisture beguiling and tantalising him.

With a muttered imprecation, he drew her down upon the settee, pressing her back until she was lying flat upon the cushions, her slender body open to his gaze as he raised his head to survey her. Her short skirt had ridden high, disclosing a bare thigh and shapely leg, and her T-shirt was tight across her breasts, showing their full curves.

Aware of his eyes ranging over her body, Tessa trembled, every part of her pulsatingly alive to his burning blue gaze. Her thighs quivered, her stomach tingled, and her breasts became heavy, tumescent, the nipples upstanding.

As the heat of desire burned between her legs, she was terribly afraid of her vulnerability to this man. Yet in a strange way she was enjoying the experience, for it showed she was capable of feelings—feelings she had occasionally doubted she possessed these past years, when she had concentrated her entire being on making a success of her career.

But now her sexual awareness of Patrick, her craving for fulfilment, showed her with a clarity she couldn't deny that work was no longer going to be enough for her. She needed a man to love, she needed to receive and to give.

She needed Patrick.

With a low moan, she lifted her arms and clasped them around his neck, aware of his tensing at her touch. He tried to pull away but she'd have none of it, half lifting herself towards him, and arching her back as she did. It was a provocative gesture and it worked, for with sudden fierceness he pushed her on to the cushions again, and fell upon her.

Tessa sank deeper into the softness, loving the weight of Patrick's body on hers, the heat of his mouth as he began kissing her again, deep, hungry kisses of consuming intensity.

His tongue was a marauder, fierce, urgent, but his searching hands were gentle, caressing her neck, lifting the T-shirt the better to cup her breasts. Impatiently his fingers sought the front fastening of her bra, deftly un-clipping it to let her breasts tumble forward, full and proud. Feeling the bare skin, he quickly pushed aside her T-shirt and began suckling her nipples, trailing his tongue from one to the other, and arousing her to such a fever-pitch of aching longing that all inhibition fled, and her own hands trailed over his muscled chest, the firm line of his back and the taut curve of his buttocks.

The swell of his arousal rose hard against her thigh, and he groaned and rubbed himself against her to ease its ache.

Her hands lowered, her fingers splaying out upon the throbbing bulge, masked by the fine black linen of his trousers.

At her touch he gasped, and, lifting his head from her breasts, trailed a moist path to the rounded indentation on the satin smoothness of her stomach.

His hands stroked her skin, his fingers gently moving lower. The waistband of her skirt restricted him, and impatiently he took his hand away and reached beneath the short hem, moving upwards over her thighs to the softly curling hair at the apex.

As his fingers twined into the tangle of hair, she gave a tremulous moan, her lips parting to nibble his ear, so hungry for him that she was conscious of nothing other than appeasement.

He muttered deep in his throat, his limbs shaking as though with fever, 'Tessa, no, we mustn't.'

'Please,' she whispered.

'No!' Wrenching himself away from her, he straightened her T-shirt and smoothed her skirt, then quickly lifted her into a sitting position. 'I must be out of my mind!' he said thickly. 'I don't know what came over me. God, I'm practically old enough to be your father!'

'I'd much rather you were my lover.'

'Don't even think it.' His expression was grim. 'You're still a kid and I should be shot for taking advantage of you.'

'How can you take advantage of me when I'm willing? I didn't push you away, did I?'

'That only makes me feel worse. You're a warm, generous-hearted girl, and——' He stopped and frowned, his eyes scanning her face. 'Too warm and too generous. If you act like this with every man who touches you, you'll——'

'I don't,' she cut in, deciding there and then to be completely truthful with him, regardless of the risk.

But she could no longer hide behind this teenage image. Or was it more sensible to wait until his undoubted attraction towards her had deepened and grown stronger, as she felt positive it would? Succumbing to temptation, she took the easy way out.

'I don't act this way with anyone else,' she reiterated.

'At least that's something,' he sighed.

'You've even fired me with ambition.'

'Indeed?'

'Yes. I'm beginning to think it's silly of me to keep bumming around instead of doing an interesting job.'

'I'm glad you're getting some sense.' As he went on regarding her, a puzzled frown marked his forehead. 'What have you done to your hair? It's different.'

'I thought you'd never notice! Do you like it?'

'Very much.' He smoothed a silky, red-gold wave from her forehead. 'It makes you look a little older.'

'I'm not a baby,' she insisted. 'Plenty of girls my age are already married.'

'Married?' As if lanced by a knife, he jumped to his feet and headed for the door. 'I must be going. It's late.'

'Not as late as all that, Patrick,' she called. 'And I don't have a rope.'

'A what?' He swung round to look at her.

'I can't lasso you and tie you to me. All I said was, some girls my age are already married, but I didn't mean *I* wanted to be.'

He swallowed visibly. 'I'm glad to hear it.'

'I'm quite prepared to be your girlfriend, though.'

'For God's sake, Tessa,' he burst out, 'don't read so much into a kiss.'

'Didn't it mean anything to you, then?'

He went to say no, then thought better of it. 'It meant enough for me to know I won't let it happen again.'

That's what *you* think, she told herself, careful to keep her face expressionless.

'About Mr Anderson's silver bowl,' Patrick said, and Tessa tensed. If he asked her once again to return it, she'd blow her top.

'Yes?' she queried, face ingenuous.

'I don't believe you took it. It *must* have been a burglar.'

She went weak with relief, and felt a surprisingly silly desire to burst into tears. 'Actually Mr Anderson took it to be mended and forgot to tell his housekeeper,' she stated.

'When did you find out?'

'When I came back from London and heard it was missing. I—er—we called him in New Zealand.'

He strode back to the couch. 'Why the hell didn't you tell me, instead of letting me think the worst of you?'

'And spoil your fun? You've always given the impression you enjoy thinking the worst of me.'

He looked ashamed, which was unusual for Patrick, and with a tentative gesture he reached out and ran the tip of one finger down the side of her cheek.

'I've never known a girl who puts me in the wrong as often as you. You're like a hair shirt to a monk.'

'You're no monk!' she replied cheekily. 'Anyway, it's good for your soul. Remember *that* under your cold shower tonight, Mr Harper.'

'I doubt if even an icy shower will do the trick!' he said drily.

Tessa hid her delight at this acknowledgement, pleased he was as vulnerable to her as she was to him.

'I think that's what I like about you,' he went on.

'My sex appeal?'

'No, your oddball humour.'

She pulled a face at him. 'One can't be passionate the whole time, and it's important to be able to laugh at the same things.'

'How worldly-wise you are.'

Tessa couldn't imagine him and Ingrid sharing a zany joke, but refrained from saying so, knowing men disliked it when women were bitchy about one another. Unfortunately her thoughts were apparent on her face, for Patrick gave her a reproving tap on the head.

'Ingrid has other qualities, my dear. Anyway, she's no competition for you.'

'Honestly?' Tessa beamed, ready to throw herself into his arms.

'Honestly. You're not long out of the schoolroom, and she and I are——'

'I know where you both are,' Tessa interrupted and would have given a great deal to know how deeply she herself had got under his skin. A moment ago she had been confident. Now she wasn't, conceding that what had happened between them this evening could have stemmed from nothing more than propinquity, and her deliberately teasing manner towards him.

'I'm not rejecting you,' he said gently. 'But we don't tread the same path, my dear, and very soon we'll be diverging completely.'

She was still thinking of a suitable answer when he closed the door behind him.

CHAPTER TWELVE

TESSA was having breakfast the next morning when there was a message from Patrick asking her to collect the china and pictures from Angus Boswell.

Pausing only for coffee, she drove into Iverton to do so, and, bowling along the country lanes, pondered on last night. How passionate yet tender Patrick had been. It was a good thing he had exercised sufficient control to call a halt, for she might well have surrendered. The knowledge frightened her, for no man had aroused her to such a degree, and it showed how deeply she cared for him.

At the moment he despised himself for being attracted to a 'kid', but once she started acting mature—as she planned to do from here on—he would realise she had more to offer than the physical, and would stop fighting against his attraction for her.

That would be the turning-point in their relationship, and within days—well, perhaps a week or two—he'd realise that life without her was unthinkable. And then she'd confess who she was.

There was no point pretending he was going to be overjoyed to learn of her career—more than a career, in fact: a deep commitment to a life-enhancing job. It meant she would always have to juggle between work, husband and children, but she had accepted this when she had entered medical school, and hoped Patrick would accept it too.

It was mid-morning before she returned from Iverton and stacked the china and paintings in the bedroom on

the second floor. Then she rushed to the kitchen to help
Eva hand out mid-morning coffee and biscuits.

It was impossible for her to restrain a leap of excitement as she entered the sitting-room and saw Patrick
talking to Jenna Donaldson and her husband. But, remembering her place, Tessa gave him a formal smile as
she approached with his coffee.

Instead of his usual grunt with barely a glance at her,
he gave her a warm smile. 'Come to my study as soon
as you've finished here,' he said. 'And tell Mrs Withers
you'll be busy with me for the rest of the day.'

Try though she did, Tessa failed to stop a tide of colour
flaming her cheeks, and with a quick nod she turned and
busied herself at the trolley, glad when everyone was
served and she could leave Eva to collect the empty cups.

'You aren't in any trouble again!' Mrs Withers exclaimed when Tessa gave her Patrick's message.

'What a funny thing to say!' she answered, and dashed
out before she was questioned further.

Patrick was impatiently pacing his study as she came
in, his chestnut-brown hair tousled, as if he'd continu-
ally raked his hand through it.

'Where have you put everything?' he asked without
preamble.

'In an empty bedroom upstairs.' She held out the key
and he took it from her with a brief smile.

'Come on, let's go and examine my new-found
fortune!'

Disappointed by his refusal to acknowledge what had
happened between them last night, she followed him to
the bedroom. She understood his anxiety to examine the
objects whose sale would buy him everything his heart
desired, but still wished he had made a reference,
however small, to their lovemaking.

Yet perhaps he was too embarrassed to do so. After
all, he hadn't yet admitted to himself that he cared for

her, though she was sure that propinquity, and the right
encouragement, would eventually make him realise it.

Eyes filled with love, she watched him scrutinise every
painting before carefully studying the Ming bowls and
vases, so absorbed by them that he was lost to everything else.

'Beats me how my great-uncle forgot all this,' he muttered. 'Yet there's no other explanation.'

'He was always a bit eccentric,' Tessa commented.

'How do you know?'

'I—er—Mrs Benson mentioned it. But surely you knew
it yourself?'

'I only met the old boy half a dozen times, and in the
last few years of his life he shut himself away and refused to see the family. I'd no idea he intended leaving
me this house. No money came with it—according to
his lawyer there wasn't any—and it was lucky I had
enough of my own to turn the Hall into my business
headquarters as well as my home. Otherwise I'd have
had to put it on the market——' Patrick broke off
sharply. 'If I had, all these things would have gone to
the new owner! I'd never have dreamt of clearing out
the attics first.' Pale-faced, he sank on to the bed. 'If
you hadn't examined everything yourself, I'd have called
in a junk man sooner or later to take the whole lot away.'

'You have to thank Mrs Withers, not me,' Tessa said,
honesty preventing her from taking the credit. 'She was
the one who asked me to look at the attics.'

'I bet she didn't tell you to open every box and carton!'

'Well, no. It was nothing other than pure nosiness on
my part!'

'What say we escort that proboscis of yours back to
the attics to see if it can sniff out other valuables?'

Springing to his feet, he strode purposefully to the
topmost floor, Tessa scurrying breathlessly after him.

'About last night,' he said abruptly as they entered one of the attics. 'It shouldn't have happened.'

'But it did.'

'To my eternal shame. You're only eighteen, for God's sake. I'm sixteen years older than you and should know better!'

'Men often fancy women years younger than themselves,' she said hurriedly. 'Only the other day I read of a man of sixty marrying a woman of forty.'

'A woman of forty knows what she's doing. Unlike you. You haven't started living yet.'

'I've lived long enough to know I love you.'

It was a bold statement, and a calculated one, though he appeared so stricken by it that she wished she'd kept her mouth shut.

'You *can't* care for me,' he said flatly. 'You're attracted to me because I'm an older man.'

'Your age has nothing to do with it. I love you because you're intelligent and interesting and——'

'Stop it! If you go on like this, you'll have to leave.'

His vehemence shocked her. 'You'd honestly send me away?'

'For *your* sake, Tessa. I can't seem to get it through your head that I enjoy my life as it is, and have no intention of complicating it with marriage.'

'I'm willing to wait until you're ready.'

'No!' It was a strangled sound. 'If I *do* marry, it will be to——' he paused, eyelids lowering '—to someone like Ingrid.'

Momentarily Tessa was lost for words. Then her brain started functioning again. He had said someone *like* Ingrid, so that didn't necessarily mean Ingrid herself. Or did it?

'You prefer blondes to redheads, then?' she managed to say lightly, her voice giving no inkling of her inner turmoil.

'Let's say I can more easily consider Ingrid than you.'

Tessa clenched her hands to hide their trembling. 'Do you kiss her the way you did me?'

Patrick gave an exasperated shake of his head. 'For heaven's sake, girl, leave things be! I've already told you what mood I was in last night. I was staggered by what Angus Boswell told me, and I went crazy with joy. I'd have kissed *any* girl who was with me. It wasn't because it was *you*. It's because you were female and provocative, and you were there!'

This was a blow to the solar plexus, but even as she felt the pain of it she wondered if Patrick meant it, or was saying it because he was worried by the supposed difference in their ages.

'I thought you fancied me,' she murmured.

'Fancying isn't love. And kissing a girl—no matter how intensely—doesn't necessarily mean more than momentary passion.'

The very quietness of his voice gave impact to what he said, and her doubts grew. Logic told her to leave the Hall and put him out of her mind, but her heart said otherwise. Besides, even if she left this instant it would take her years to forget him, so why not stay and hope that proximity would work its magic?

'OK,' she shrugged. 'You've made your feelings clear and I'll accept it.'

'You mean that?'

'Sure. There are plenty more fish in the sea.'

Wry humour lit his eyes, enhancing the blue, but he said nothing, and silently bent to prise open a rusty tin trunk.

For the next few hours they worked side by side, Patrick's agile hands making short shrift of locked cases and nailed lids. It didn't take them long to discover that three of the attics held only rubbish, though it was another story in the fourth, which disclosed a set of six

Elizabethan glass goblets, date-marked 1582, and a large leather jewel case containing two suede pouches: one filled with inch-square, flawless emeralds, and the other with glistening black pearls.

'This is the most fantastic haul I . . .' Lost for words, Patrick sank on to the top of a wooden case.

'There's one trunk left to open,' Tessa reminded him. 'I suggest we stop for lunch and carry on afterwards.'

'You go and eat. I'm not hungry.'

The rumble emanating from his stomach gave the lie to this, and, flinging him a baleful glance, she went off to make some sandwiches.

Returning with a thermos of coffee, and a plate piled high with food, she found Patrick bent over the opened trunk, his expression bemused.

'What else have you found?' she asked, setting the plate and thermos on the floor.

'Mmm.'

'I can't decipher that! Lift it up and show me.'

'It's too heavy.'

'Solid lead?' she asked sarcastically.

'No, solid gold!'

'You're kidding!'

But Patrick wasn't. An eighteen-inch-high gold Buddha, inset with hundreds of precious stones, the largest of which was a glowing ruby the size of a pigeon's egg, gazed serenely up at her.

'Jeepers!' she gasped.

'My sentiments entirely!' Dropping to the floor, Patrick reached for a sandwich. 'The Finworth family obviously enjoyed collecting little baubles!'

She giggled, and began to eat. 'Decorative trifles that could probably clear the National Debt!'

Grinning at each other, they munched their way through the laden plate, and drained the thermos.

'Best meal I've eaten in years,' he commented, wiping his hands on the napkin she had remembered to bring with her.

'Me too.' She yawned and stretched.

'You must be tired,' he said. 'You were digging round here most of yesterday, and now today.'

'It's worth digging when you find treasure!'

'Even though the treasure isn't yours?'

'It makes no odds. It's the finding that's exciting.'

'What a typical Tessa remark,' he said gently, the softening of his face giving her such hope that she realised she couldn't carry on her game.

'There's something I have to tell you, Patrick. I'm not—— '

'What on earth are you two doing here?'

They turned to see Ingrid coming towards them, carefully stepping over mounds of dusty paper. Without waiting for them to answer, she peered into the trunk.

'Good gracious!' She glanced round at Patrick. 'Pity it isn't real. If it were, it would be worth a fortune.'

'I'd say the ruby will fetch half a million,' Patrick murmured casually.

'The ruby?' Ingrid clutched at his arm, her pale eyes wide with astonishment. 'You—you mean the Buddha's for *real*?'

'Every ingot of him!'

'That's incredible! Why, you—you'll be able to buy into Allinson's company! Better still, you can buy out one of his rivals!'

'If I sold everything we've found, I might even manage a chunk of IBM!'

Catching a dumbfounded Ingrid by the arm, Patrick showed her the jewel box and the goblets, then told her of the paintings and china.

The girl glowed with pleasure, her pale skin pink, her usually cool eyes flashing with excitement. Always beautiful, she was now entrancing, and Tessa, watching Patrick eye Ingrid, decided not to tell him the truth about herself just yet.

Despondency swamped her. It was a rare feeling, for she was a fighter by nature. Yet, observing Ingrid's silver-blonde head on a level with Patrick's mouth, she conceded it was stupid to kid herself that five feet one was as alluring as five eight.

'Shall I help you go through the other cases?' Ingrid was asking.

'No, thanks, we've finished. I'm going to stack this lot with the other stuff, then ask Christie's to come and assess it.'

'You'd better call John Allinson too, and say you can buy those shares he offered you.'

'Not till I find out exactly what all the things are worth.'

'It's silly to wait. The paintings alone will more than pay for your stake!'

'I still want Christie's' opinion.'

'Very well.' Ingrid's casual tone was at odds with her tightly clenched hands, though Tessa was the only one to notice them.

'If you've finished helping Mr Harper,' the girl said to her from the doorway, 'you can give Pedro a hand cleaning the silver.'

'I need her hand here!' Patrick interposed, and with a shrug Ingrid left them.

'Thanks for rescuing me. She knows darn well I hate cleaning silver!'

'More than you hate taking orders from her?'

'Only because she's always on my back.'

'Probably because she thinks if she wasn't, you'd be on your backside!'

'If you're suggesting I'm lazy——' Tessa flared, her anger abating as she saw Patrick's amusement.

'I enjoy riling you,' he confessed. 'And I dare say Ingrid does too. If you were more mature, you wouldn't rise to her bait.'

'If *she* were more mature, she wouldn't cast it at me!'

He laughed, but Tessa was too cross to join in. None the less, his advice was sound, though hard to follow. Normally she'd be amused by anyone as pointedly jealous as Ingrid. But normality appeared to go out of the window when love came in at the door!

'Stop breathing fire and brimstone and put your energies to better use,' Patrick ordered, lifting the leather jewel box and heading for the bedroom below.

Two days later, the experts arrived to make their assessment, and, after a week of nail-biting tension for everyone concerned, gave Patrick an astronomical evaluation.

Realising the impossibility of keeping the news secret, and that the media were going to descend on him like a pack of vultures, Patrick took himself to America to visit John Allinson, leaving Ingrid to deal with the Press and television cameras that parked themselves in the driveway.

Tessa, anxious not to be photographed, feigned a severe attack of food poisoning, and remained closeted in Greentrees, first warning Mr and Mrs Withers not to mention the part she had played in discovering the treasure trove.

Although surprised that she didn't wish to become a ten-day celebrity, they promised not to mention her, as did Ingrid, who was only too happy for her to be kept out of the news.

It was tedious being penned in the house, but Tessa was too scared to go in the garden in case a roving newshound spied her, and came across to obtain a 'neighbour's opinion of the greatest art finds of the century'.

But finally the furore died, the media departed, and Tessa went back to the Hall, ostensibly recovered.

'You timed your return well,' Mrs Withers greeted her. 'Mr Patrick flew home last night.'

'How is he?'

'Fine. Wait till you see the present he brought me. A pure cashmere coat. Soft as butter and fit for a queen! Said it was a "thank-you" for making you clear out the attics!'

The intercom buzzed and Pedro answered it. 'The boss wants you in the library, Tessa. On the treble.'

'On the double!' she corrected, heart racing madly as she dashed out.

The sight of Patrick's tall, lean body, a newly acquired tan making his eyes bluer than ever, did nothing to calm her, and she took several deep breaths.

'I heard you were ill,' he said by way of greeting.

'It was nothing. I'm fit as a flea now.'

And indeed she was, so delighted he was within touching distance that she was buoyant with happiness. Their eyes met, hers limpid with love, his enigmatic. Then he moved back and pointed to three large packages by the wall.

'For you. A little thank-you to be going on with.'

'It wasn't necessary,' she said uncomfortably.

'I think it was. If you don't like it, I'll change it.'

But it was impossible not to like the quadraphonic music centre, for it was exactly what a girl of her supposed age would go overboard for. Idly she wondered what he'd have given her had he known her true persona, for he had clearly taken great pains in choosing this particular gift.

Tears were close, and she kept her head lowered. 'It's lovely, Patrick—Mr Harper.'

'Stick with Patrick,' he said gruffly. 'I think we're sufficiently well acquainted for that.'

Instantly she raised her eyes to his, but he hastily averted his gaze, showing her he was still determined to fight his attraction to her.

'I'll have Withers take the present home for you this evening,' he went on.

'There's no need. I'll collect it in Unc—in Mr Anderson's car.'

Her delight in the gift lessened considerably when, later that day, she saw the aquamarine pendant he had given Ingrid. She didn't begrudge the girl, but was miserably aware that it was a much more personal gift than her own.

What if she was misjudging Patrick's feelings, and he had only made love to her because she had provoked him and was available? Why, he had actually said as much, but she had refused to believe him! Now she wasn't sure.

From what she had gleaned of his past from Mrs Withers, it was littered with discarded girlfriends, and who was to say his future was going to be different? Trouble was, her love for him had made her forget she might only be a single pearl in a long string of pearls which he had strung along and dropped by the wayside.

Apart from Ingrid, of course, who was a constant in his life.

Patrick and Ingrid. Ingrid and Patrick. It was a refrain that haunted her throughout a sleepless night, and when she went to the Hall next morning there were violet shadows beneath her eyes.

'You look as if you were listening to the music centre all night,' Patrick joked when she took in his morning post.

She nodded, wondering how he'd react if she said her sleeplessness was due to him.

'Incidentally, I'd like to give you something more.'

'Definitely not.'

'I was thinking of an art appreciation course,' he went on as if she hadn't spoken. 'Sotheby's do an excellent one, and with the right training you might end up working for them. Unless you'd rather take an arts degree?'

His anxiety to help her find a career was touching, but she didn't show it. 'Still trying to educate me?'

'Is that wrong?'

'It's wrong for *me*.'

'Why? You have a keen eye for what's genuine, and with the proper training you——'

'Will become head of Sotheby's Art Department!'

'Why not?'

She suddenly decided to play him along. 'OK, then, let's say I make it to the top and become picture advisor to the Queen! But what happens if the next man I fall in love with is like you, and doesn't want his wife to have a career?'

Patrick's silky dark eyebrows drew together, and she was amused at snaring him in his own trap. But he was too wily to be caught for long, and, leaning back in his chair, he shook his head at her.

'*My* mother was a physiotherapist until she married, and I can assure you she never regretted giving it up.'

'We're talking of *today's* woman,' Tessa countered. 'If I'd worked my guts out to get somewhere, I wouldn't give it up in exchange for a wedding ring! Anyway, women can hold down a job *and* be loving wives and mothers.'

'But at what cost? When they're home they're worried stiff that they're losing out in their career, and when they're working they feel guilty at leaving their children.' Patrick shook his head, a lock of dark hair falling forward. 'Dammit, you already know my views on this subject.'

Mischievously, she decided to do a complete turn-about.

'I'm glad you think like that,' she said in a little-girl voice. 'You see, I've only been sticking up for career women to provoke you.'

'You do that without *trying*,' came the wry response.

'What I—what I mean is that, when I marry, I'm going to devote my entire life to my husband.'

Patrick gaped at her. 'You will?'

'Absolutely. It's so fulfilling to look after one's home and family. I want at least three children.'

'I'm one of five,' he said.

'Er—five sounds ideal.'

'It's wonderful,' he enthused.

'It is?'

'Of course six is better, and if you'd agree to seven I'd marry you myself.'

'Seven?' she echoed hollowly.

'On the other hand, it would be a great pity to deprive the stage of such a magnificent actress. You make Sarah Bernhardt seem like Minnie Mouse!'

'Oh!' Scarlet-faced, Tessa searched for a retort.

Not that she was given a chance to find one, for with an angry stride he was in front of her. 'You're the most infuriating, exasperating, irritating——'

'Oh, Patrick!' Unable to stop herself, she melted into his arms.

He tried to draw back, but it was no more than a token resistance, for the feel of her soft body was his undoing, and with an incoherent murmur he lowered his head to find her mouth.

Pressing herself close to him, she felt the throbbing swell and arched her body against it. Instantly he groaned, his grip on her tightening as he pulled her closer and his lips parted hers. Frenziedly his tongue pen-etrated the sweet moistness of her mouth, filling it with his own sweetness, the guttural sounds deep in his throat indicating his fierce longing to penetrate her in other, more intimate ways.

She slid her hands down his back, kneading the steely muscles and feeling them quiver at her touch. It gave her a sense of power, and triumph coursed through her, routing her nervousness and spurring her to glide gentle fingers along his thighs, curving round the strong hip-bones to rest on the leaping, alive muscle pressing hard and urgently against her.

She was incapable of thought, conscious only of the present, spinning higher and higher into a vortex of ecstasy that only ceased as a harsh voice stopped her spinning, and hard hands shook her into reality.

Opening her eyes, she stared into Patrick's face, loving the sheen of sweat on the tightly stretched skin that covered his high cheekbones, and the sensuous fullness of the beautifully curved mouth. But she didn't love what the mouth was saying.

'For God's sake, Tessa, stop trying to seduce me!'

'I'm not.'

'Then you're giving a darn good imitation! You threw yourself at me.'

'It took you quite a while to object!'

'What do you expect when you clung to me like instant glue! This has got to stop. I told you before I went to the States that I don't play games with little girls.'

'I don't want you to play,' she entreated. 'Make it for real.'

'No! Can't you get it into your head that it won't work? Apart from bed, we don't want the same things.'

'Then you *do* want me!' she cried.

Lowered lids obscured the bright blue eyes. 'I'm a red-blooded man; what do you expect? But desire is no basis for a relationship.'

'It's a beginning.'

'And it would have a quick end!' Side-stepping her, he went to the door and opened it. 'Please go.'

She trembled. 'Go? For good?'

'That wasn't what I meant,' he confessed wryly, 'but it would be for *your* good if you did.'

'I don't want to leave.'

He hesitated, then sighed. 'A word of warning, then. If you plan to re-enact this scene, don't! Fling yourself at me again, and you'll be out on your ear faster than a bullet from a gun!'

CHAPTER THIRTEEN

FOR the next few days, all Tessa thought about was how it was going to end between herself and Patrick. Dolefully she admitted she was between the devil and the deep blue sea.

As long as he thought her an eighteen-year-old, he'd swallow his tongue before admitting he loved her. Yet she couldn't confess her real age without revealing she was a surgeon—and then she wouldn't see him for dust!

Like it or not, she had to stick with her original plan and carry on as she was, hoping that when she finally came clean he'd be so besotted with her that he wouldn't object to her continuing her career.

Trouble was, she would be fit enough to return to the hospital in another few weeks, and her conscience wouldn't allow her to stay on longer. Still, a lot could happen in that time—if she played her cards right!

Dreamily she gave herself over to foolish romantic thoughts, quivering with pleasure as she recalled the desire in Patrick's eyes when he looked at her when they were alone.

But who was the desire for? The carefree girl he thought her to be, or the passionate woman she became when she was in his arms? She frowned. Wasn't he aware of the difference between Tessa the teenager and the mature woman who answered him back kiss for kiss? So far he hadn't noticed the discrepancy, and ruefully she wondered if all men were as blind.

She went into the kitchen to prepare tea. Withers and his good lady were off for the afternoon, but cold meat

and salad were in the refrigerator for dinner, and all Tessa
had to do was make afternoon tea.

She was placing a chocolate cake on the trolley when
there was a telephone call from Bobby. Luckily she was
alone in the kitchen, but she still kept her voice low.

'How did you know where to find me?'

'I called your daily, and she gave me your godfather's
number. An old bird answered, and when I said I had
to speak to you urgently she gave me this number. You
got two country homes, or are you stashing up with a
boyfriend?'

'Clever of you to guess!' she teased. 'But why the urgency to speak to me?'

'I'm off to Brazil for two months. Some millionaire
rancher called the gallery and asked if I'd do a frieze of
a polo scene in his living-room. Gray said the price he
offered was too good to refuse.'

As always, Tessa was amused at hearing the kind-
hearted but austere Graham Koster referred to as Gray.
Bobby must be the only one of his artists who dared call
him that!

'Twenty-five thousand quid, plus expenses, ain't hay!'
Bobby was saying.

'It certainly isn't,' she gasped. 'Will it delay the new
show you're preparing?'

'Nope. My side of it's done, and the rest is up to Jack.
I'll just have to put the finishing touches to a few things
when I get back.'

'Don't forget to send me a card!'

'I may send you an invitation! I'm being loaned a guest
house of my own.'

'Don't tempt me.'

Tessa was smiling as she replaced the receiver, and
only as she swung round to the trolley did she see Patrick
leaning against the kitchen lintel.

As always, he was casually but expensively dressed. No untidy, stoop-shouldered boffin this one, but a tall, slim man who might have stepped from the pages of *Vogue*. He must have had a swim not long ago, too, for his hair clung damply to his head, the warm chestnut colour deep as mahogany.

'A call from the boyfriend?' he asked, arms folded across his chest.

'A friend,' she corrected.

'A loving one, by the sound of it.'

'A very loving one, but not the way you mean.' The electric kettle boiled, and with relief she turned to it. 'Will you have tea in your study, or in the sitting-room with the others?'

'I'll have it in here. Then I must pack.'

'Where are you going?'

'To the States. I'm leaving first thing in the morning.'

'That's sudden.'

'I apologise. It quite slipped my mind that I had to acquaint you with my movements!'

'You're very interested in what *I* do.'

'I'm interested in what you get up to.' He was the one to do the correcting this time. 'You're a mischievous baggage, young lady, and have to be watched!'

'I'm happy for you to watch me any day!' Intentionally she licked her tongue delicately across her lower lip.

'Stop that, Tessa. I'm not going to let you seduce me again.'

'Scared you won't know when to stop?'

'Scared *you* won't. And promiscuity is dangerous.'

'Just because I respond to you, it doesn't mean I'm promiscuous.'

'In addition,' he continued as if she hadn't spoken, 'if it's marriage you're after, don't all the women's magazines say it's better to keep a man wanting than to give in to him?'

'I haven't given in to you, have I?'

'I haven't asked you to!'

Only for a brief instant did Tessa hesitate before saying, 'You're right. If you did, I'd say yes.'

A flame glowed in his eyes, then he swiftly averted his head and straddled a chair by the table. 'Little girls shouldn't act the temptress.'

'I'm not acting. I mean it.'

'Stop it, Tessa,' he reiterated.

His tone brooked no argument, and she cooled the situation. Anyway, with his imminent departure, now wasn't the time to hot it up!

'Fancy a piece of cake?' she asked brightly.

'Make it a cheese sandwich and you're on. But not the doorsteps you cut me once before!'

Silently she took out a loaf of bread and sliced off several thin slices.

'Good work,' he teased. 'You've certainly improved with a knife!'

She hid a smile, then boldly said, 'When I was a kid I fancied being a surgeon.'

He laughed. 'A tree surgeon most likely—never bodies!'

'I'll wipe the smile off your face one day, Patrick Harper.'

'Only if I'm on an operating table and you're holding the scalpel!'

Here was her golden opportunity, but because he was leaving in a few hours she was unwilling to take it.

'The sandwich,' Patrick reminded her.

Hurriedly she slapped on two slices of cheddar cheese, topped them with a pickle, and passed the sandwich across to him.

'Let me drive you to the airport,' she blurted out.

'I'm going with Ingrid.'

Did he mean she was going to the States too? Tessa swallowed the question.

'Don't be possessive.' Patrick read her expression correctly. 'Ingrid isn't coming with me, but if she were it wouldn't be any business of yours.'

'I simply think you can do better.'

'And *I* think you should stop interfering in my life. A few weeks from now your replacement will be taking over, and once you're among your friends I'll be part of your lively and interesting past!'

'I'd rather you were part of my present.' She met his gaze steadily, though it grew less steady as she felt herself drowning in the deep blue depths. She trembled and her lips parted, moist with longing.

'I told you to stop that!' he said thickly, and, plate in hand, stalked from the room.

With Patrick away, Tessa found Ingrid so bossy that she feigned summer flu and stayed home. But she called Emmy every day to see how things were going, and when she learned Patrick was due back the following Tuesday she judiciously returned to the Hall on the Monday.

'If you're expecting to be paid for your absence, you'll have to bring me a letter from your doctor,' Ingrid snapped as they passed each other in the butler's pantry.

Tessa nodded, speculating on the girl's reaction if she wrote her own note and presented it.

'What's the joke?' Ingrid demanded.

'Nothing.'

'Then stop grinning and get on with your work.'

Waving a duster under Ingrid's nose, Tessa scurried away.

That night she dreamed of Patrick, and awoke with a deep urge to press her body to his, to feel the touch of his skin on every part of her, to twine her legs around his hard thighs and press the silken triangle of her womanhood to his throbbing masculine one. A flame of desire licked her, almost as though it were his tongue, and she clasped the pillow tightly.

I love you, Patrick Harper! she cried silently as she drifted off to sleep again. If only I knew how to make you admit you feel the same about me.

The next day, knowing he was flying the Atlantic, she did her chores with a lighter heart, counting the hours till he was due home. There was little enough to occupy her, for no one was off duty or sick, and after lunch was cleared she idled away the afternoon.

If it weren't for Ingrid she would have gone for a swim, for when Patrick was away the pool was at his staff's disposal. But if the Swedish girl saw her enjoying herself in the water, she'd soon find her an unpleasant job to do!

Yet, the more Tessa thought of the pool, the hotter and stickier she felt, and at five o'clock she went into the staff cloakroom, donned a bikini under her dress, and set off for the west wing garden. In another half-hour she was off duty, and if Ingrid found her before, tough luck!

The sun was hot and the pool a blue oasis sparkling under a paler blue sky. Dropping her dress on a lounger, she padded over to the side and dived in, a flash of scarlet bikini against milk-white skin.

The water was refreshingly cold, and she cavorted in it like a dolphin, feeling her tension ebb, her tightened nerves uncoil. Soon Patrick would be home, and at the earliest opportunity she'd set the record straight, then try to convince him she could make him happy and continue her career at one and the same time.

She refused to believe he was as rigid in his opinions as he stated. After all, he was a man of the world, and knew that these days more and more marriages had both partners working, even when there was no financial necessity for the woman to do so.

Tessa was floating in the centre of the pool when Ingrid's voice—hard and strident since Patrick was not around to hear it—asked what she was doing there.

'I'll give you three guesses!' Tessa answered, straightening and treading water.

'I'm clever enough to need only one! You're wasting time—as you often do.'

'Come off it.' Tessa was not about to give in to further bullying. By tomorrow Ingrid would know exactly who she was, and feeling knee-high to a grasshopper. 'I've no more work and fancied a swim.'

'This isn't a hotel. If you're finished for the day, you should leave.'

'I was waiting to see Mr Harper.'

'Why should you imagine he wants to see *you*?'

It was a good question, bearing in mind their last conversation. But Tessa pushed it aside.

'Anyway,' Ingrid continued, 'he won't be here this evening. I'm meeting him at the airport and we're staying in town.'

'Why?' Tessa asked involuntarily.

'Because he has an early morning meeting there, and it will save his getting up at the crack of dawn. Not that it's any business of yours,' Ingrid added for good measure.

The pleasurable sense of anticipation Tessa had felt all day ebbed, her hopes—high a moment ago—in ruins.

She didn't blame Ingrid for doing her best to worm her way into Patrick's personal life, but she was furious with Patrick for allowing it to happen when she was positive he didn't care for the girl. If this was his way of showing she herself meant nothing to him, then he had done it as hurtfully as possible.

As soon as Ingrid was out of sight, Tessa towelled herself dry and went home. An idea had taken root, and she examined it carefully. If she drove to the airport immediately, she might manage to tell Patrick who she really was before Ingrid arrived to collect him. Confessing her story in the hurly burly of the Arrivals Hall wasn't exactly the best way of gaining his attention or understanding, though, and she'd do better to wait till tomorrow. Yet if she did, it meant another miserable night for her, with her imagination working overtime as she envisaged Ingrid in Patrick's bed. But better that than to be too precipitate.

'Waiting for one more day won't make things worse,' she told herself aloud. 'He may have said Ingrid would make a better wife for him than you, but it doesn't mean he's already sampled the goods! Why, he as good as told you he isn't having an affair with her.'

But, no matter how often Tessa repeated this, the green-eyed demon of jealousy remained on her shoulder, and, walking to the Hall the next morning, she felt as if she had been squeezed through a mangle.

Her mood was not improved by discovering she had lost her watch. In her fury against Ingrid she must have left it by the pool. She dashed across the lawn to get it, but, though she searched for it high and low, it wasn't there. Perhaps someone had used the pool after her and found it.

A quick word with Mike and the others elicited no joy, and Pedro's pronouncement that he had chased a couple of boys off the grounds last night decided her she had lost it for good.

She was both angry and upset. Though fully insured, the watch had been a gift from Uncle Martin, and precious to her.

This bad news was compounded by learning that Patrick and Ingrid were staying over in London another day.

Tessa reminded herself she wasn't his keeper, and he was free to do as he liked with whom he liked. But why oh, why did it have to be with Ingrid? How much easier to bear her jealousy if he were with another woman. After all, he was single and, if determined to prove she herself meant nothing to him, what better way than to find someone else? But Ingrid? Give her an inch, and she'd take a mile!

The day dragged by on leaden feet, and Tessa was glad when Withers sent her home early. Another miserable night faced her, and she rose at five a.m. to go for a jog.

Luckily her looks didn't pity her, for excitement at seeing Patrick brought a flush to her cheeks, their pink matching the cambric cotton dress she'd bought on her shopping spree.

His car, containing Patrick with Ingrid beside him, was drawing to a stop by the front door as Tessa came down the driveway, and at once the sun shone for her again. However, it dimmed as he climbed out and she saw the dark shadows under his eyes, for they conjured up an unwelcome picture of nocturnal activity!

'Was your trip successful?' she managed to ask.

'Very.'

'May I talk to you alone?' she questioned softly.

'I've a mass of things to do. Later maybe.' He walked past her at a run.

Tessa went equally fast to the kitchen, though not fast enough to miss the expression on Ingrid's face as she followed more slowly on his heels, smug as a woman heading the queue at a Harrods sale!

Throughout the morning Tessa waited to see Patrick, but it was well into the afternoon before she was summoned to his study.

He was still in his city suit, indicating he had worked full stretch since returning home. Yet he no longer appeared tired, and she guessed that, like herself, he found hidden reserves when his workload demanded it. One more thing—among so many—that they had in common. If only she could make him realise it.

She gave him a wide smile. 'I'm glad you're back, Patrick. I missed you very much.'

He scowled. 'Only because you don't have enough to occupy you. You shouldn't have taken the job at Greentrees.'

'I met *you* through it.'

'That's another reason why!'

'But——'

'No buts, Tessa, and no arguments. I made it quite plain what the position was between us before I went to the States, and I haven't changed my mind. I only called you in here to give you this.'

This was a small, beautifully wrapped package, and, anticipating an expensive little trinket, she was struck dumb to find a double row of shimmering pearls. Real ones.

'Like it?' he asked.

'It's beautiful,' she gasped. 'But I—I can't accept it.' She closed the case and held it out to him.

'Don't be childish. I want you to have it. It's because of you I found a fortune. I still have nightmares when I remember how close a junk man came to getting it!'

'I don't need payment for what I did. Anyway, you've already given me a stereo. That was generous enough.'

'And I want you to have the pearls too. Regard it as a gift from my company, if you prefer it,' he added, noticing her mutinous expression. 'Quit arguing, girl, and put it on.'

Reluctant, she stood there doing nothing, and he took the pearls from her hand, put them round her neck and closed the diamond clasp. Then he drew her over to a small Chippendale mirror and pivoted her to face it.

The alabaster of her skin reflected the luminous glow of the pearls, their coolness quickly warming as his nearness made the blood pound in her body. She gave a tremulous sigh. If only he'd encompass her the way his gift encompassed her throat! Her eyes met his in the mirror, and it was as if he read her thought, for a spark of flame lit the blue depths, and his lower lip moved slightly. But he said nothing, and silently stepped back from her.

'Patrick, I——'

She broke off as Ingrid came in, her rap on the door in unison with her entry. Quick as a flash the pale eyes homed in on the pearls, then went to Patrick.

'I hope I'm not interrupting you?' she asked.

'No,' Patrick said.

'Yes,' said Tessa.

Ingrid's lips curved in an arc of amusement, and if Patrick saw it he pretended not to as he returned to the chair behind his desk.

'I was giving Tessa a thank-you gift. Perhaps you can persuade her she deserves it. She seems to believe she doesn't.'

'Of course you do, my dear.' Ingrid favoured her with a honeyed smile. 'It's childish to be modest about what you did. Accept the gift and enjoy it.'

Mutely applauding the girl's acting ability—it was as good as her own!—Tessa shrugged. 'I can't see myself having any use for a necklace like this. It's far too grand to go with jeans and T-shirt!'

'Look on it as a nest-egg and put it in the bank,' Patrick interpolated.

'I'm sure you'll find an occasion to wear pearls,' Ingrid said dulcetly. 'I think they'll go well with your Rolex.' She slipped her hand into her pocket and drew out Tessa's watch. 'I popped back to the pool after you'd gone the other day, and found it on the grass.'

'Thank goodness.' Tessa reached for it, and slipped it round her wrist. 'I was afraid I'd lost it.'

'I hope Tessa doesn't believe *my* gift's a Hong Kong copy,' Patrick chuckled.

'This isn't a copy,' Ingrid trilled, her perfectly arched eyebrows rising. 'It's worth a couple of thousand pounds at least.'

Patrick went motionless, and Tessa wished the ground would open and swallow her.

'Will you leave us alone, Ingrid?' he requested.

'Of course.'

With a gracious nod she went out, and, as the door closed on her, Patrick's hard blue gaze probed Tessa's face.

'Where did you get it?' he asked quietly.

'I didn't steal it, if that's what you're implying!'

'I never suggested you did. I merely want to know where you got it.'

Here was the opportunity Tessa was looking for, and, drawing a steadying breath, she took it.

'Mr Anderson gave it to me. He's——'

'What?' Patrick roared. 'Why you rotten little—— '

'Oh, do be quiet, and let me explain,' Tessa shouted back. 'You see, I'm——'

'I see very well what you are!' he blazed. 'A cheap gold-digger!'

'I'm not a gold-digger!'

'And you're certainly not cheap!' he added.

'If you'll shut up a minute, I can——'

'Invent another fantasy to fool me with? Forget it. Everything you've ever told me has been a lie. You said you hadn't met Mr Anderson till he gave you a job, and now you expect me to believe he gave you a watch worth thousands? What did you have to do to get it? Make eyes at him the way you've been doing to me? Is that why you make a play for older men? Because they're easier victims?'

Grim-faced, he strode to the door, pushing her so roughly aside as she went to stop him that she slipped and crashed to the floor. Before she could rise to run after him, he disappeared from sight.

Grimacing with pain, she got to her feet and headed for his sitting-room. But he wasn't there, and she hurried into the main house.

'There you are,' Ingrid observed, emerging from the computer-room and closing the door behind her. 'There's no need for you to stay on any longer today. Mr Harper's going through one of the new software programs with Mike, and we'll be delaying dinner till nine.'

'Suits me. I've no objection to working late.'

'How conscientious of you! But it isn't necessary.' A pale hand came up to smooth the silver-blonde hair. 'I do hope I didn't embarrass you about your watch. If I had known you'd pretended it wasn't real, I wouldn't have mentioned that it was.'

'Forgive me if I don't believe you!'

'You think I want to get you into trouble?'

'Damn right I do.'

'Foolish girl.' Ingrid's lip curled pityingly. 'Don't you know how unimportant you are to me?'

'Then why have you been so anxious to get rid of me?'

'Because you're an embarrassment to Mr Harper, and the sooner you leave for good, the better.'

It was all Tessa could do not to blurt out her identity. But Patrick had to be told first, and, swallowing her anger, she marched to the front door.

'You'll soon have your wish, Miss Mortensen. After tomorrow I won't be a Girl Friday, and I definitely won't be your general dogsbody!'

CHAPTER FOURTEEN

WITH no chance of seeing Patrick till morning, Tessa did her best to relax, but, going to bed after a warm bath, she found herself staring through the window at the dark bulk of Finworth Hall, its lights glimmering through the trees.

Maybe she would stroll over. If she struck lucky she might catch Patrick by the pool—he often went for a late-night swim. Slipping out of her nightdress and into a cotton skirt and blouse, she tiptoed from the house.

The moon lit her way, a million stars sparkling above her. Lifting her face to the sky, she felt herself to be a microcosm in the universe, yet even if she was infinitesimal, her love for Patrick was immense. It was inconceivable that they wouldn't eventually share a life together.

Speeding across the grass, she peeped through the windows of the computer-room. Only Jenna Donaldson and her husband were there, and as she watched they switched off the lights and went out.

She set off for the pool. It was deserted, a solitary lamp throwing a pale glow over the water, but through the drawn curtains of Patrick's sitting-room she glimpsed a warmer light, and moved towards it, her canvas shoes soundless on the York stone terrace.

Poor darling, he must still be working. She had no right to disturb him, yet it was unthinkable to turn back without confessing the truth regarding the watch, and Uncle Martin's being her godfather.

Should she say what she had to say baldly, or lead up to it? She sighed. Regardless of how she planned it, it would take its own course. Yet the end result would be the same: Patrick was going to be livid, until his sense of humour got the better of him and he saw the funny side of the whole episode.

More importantly, he would admit he loved her, and accept her career.

Excitement burgeoned, threatening to overwhelm her, and she ached to call his name, to see his face as he realised how badly he had misjudged her this afternoon. Almost affectionately she tapped the watch on her wrist. He would fall over himself with contrition when he remembered his cruel remarks. Gold-digger indeed!

Eyes sparkling mischievously, she reached the french windows. The curtains were almost drawn, and, wishing to savour the sight of him, she moved forward and peeped through a chink in the brocade.

Burning the midnight oil? Working on a problem? Who was she fooling? The strength seeped from her, paralysing all movement. It couldn't be true. She wasn't seeing straight!

Closing her eyes, she squeezed them tight, then opened them again. But nothing had changed and she found herself staring at the same scene—Patrick lying on the settee with Ingrid in his arms!

White-hot fury engulfed Tessa, and she wanted to yell and scream. But no sound emerged from her dry throat, and she remained mute, and motionless as a statue. Yet could a statue bleed, cry, shatter into a thousand pieces and still remain intact? She gazed down at herself, surprised to find she was the same, when she knew she would never be the same again.

How blind she was, so busy playing her own game against Patrick that she had never realised he was playing a sadistic game with *her*. His jealousy of her was nothing but male ego!

Tessa wanted to walk away from the window, but masochism impelled her to stay, watching as pale arms wrapped themselves round a bronzed neck, and pulled the wide-shouldered, muscular body down upon the slender one. She saw the avid red mouth press itself on a mouth that had once voraciously drunk from hers, and the soft moan of pain that escaped her came from the very depths of her being.

Blindly she turned and ran back the way she had come, prey to a thousand bitter thoughts, though the bitterest was the admission of her stupidity.

Once in her room, anger took over. Patrick was a swine to have made love to her when he was having an affair with Ingrid. She would have respected him more him if he had bluntly admitted it.

True, he had told her not to try to seduce him, even occasionally made a half-hearted attempt not to kiss her, but if he had genuinely wished to dissuade her from making a play for him he would have come clean about Ingrid. Much as she hated admitting it, he was having two women on a string.

Now that she understood the reason for Ingrid's bitchiness to her, her anger against the girl faded. She almost felt sorry for her for not realising what a woman-iser Patrick was! Or did she believe that if she hung around long enough he would eventually marry her? Whether or not he did, he wasn't going to be faithful to her. A man who enjoyed two-timing women wasn't the steadfast kind.

Only one thing was certain. *She* wasn't going to be around to witness what happened.

Pacing her bedroom, Tessa considered whether to walk away from the entire situation without saying goodbye. She was sorely tempted, but decided it was the coward's

way out. Besides, it would give her great pleasure to disclose her identity and cut Patrick down to size.

Strange to remember this had been her initial intention
when first embarking on her charade, though the cut
wouldn't have been a painful one, merely a little nick
to warn him not to judge people by their appearances.
But now she determined to cut him deeply, and she toyed
with a hundred ways of making him suffer, each one
more painful than the last.

Finally, exhausted by her rage, she sat by the window,
watching the moon glide across the sky and dawn slowly
send pink and lemon fingers across the lightening blue.
As colours took form, her rage faded, replaced by a resolve to carry on with her life and not allow him to make
her bitter.

A few hours ago she had believed her world was at
an end, but she saw this wasn't true. Using her skill as
a surgeon to make people well was still supremely important to her and, once immersed in her work, she
would regain her perspective and realise Patrick wasn't
the only man in the world for her.

Fine words, she reflected bleakly, for he was the only
man in *her* world.

'You're pale as a ghost,' Mrs Benson greeted her next
morning. 'Not having a relapse, are you?'

'No. Just a lousy night.'

'You're working too hard at the Hall. You came here
for a rest, but you've done nothing except rush back and
forth like a demented hen!'

'I won't be rushing in future,' Tessa stated. 'I'm returning to London. I'm fit enough to work and the hospital needs me.'

'A bit sudden, this decision?'

'Not really. I've thought about it for days.'

'I wish I were a fly on the wall when you make your
confession to Mr Harper!'

'I don't plan to tell him.'

Mrs Benson's mouth fell open. 'Why not? Is anything wrong?'

At the concern on the woman's motherly face, Tessa almost confided in her. Yet if she did, she would burst into tears, and she was damned if she was going to shed any more over Patrick.

'What began as a joke doesn't seem funny any longer,' she murmured. 'I'm going to give in my notice and quietly disappear.'

'What will happen when you come here again? You're bound to bump into Mr Harper sooner or later.'

'I'll cross that bridge when I come to it,' Tessa hedged, reluctant to say that when she did visit her godfather she'd make sure she remained within the confines of the house and garden.

Mrs Withers was as astonished as Mrs Benson to learn she was leaving the Hall. 'But the woman Mr Patrick engaged isn't starting for another month.'

'I'm sure you can manage without me,' Tessa said brightly.

'That's as maybe. But you seemed so happy here.'

'I was. But I won't be if I stay on. I'm bored with country life, and fancy moving back to London.'

'I dare say it's too quiet here for a bright young girl like you. It's time you started thinking of your future. When are you leaving?'

'Today.'

'Don't believe in giving much notice, do you?'

Wishing it were possible to go this very second, Tessa forced a smile. 'You know how inconsiderate the young are!'

'Get away with you!' Mrs Withers scolded. 'You're a kind-hearted girl, and thoughtful too. It's my guess Miss Mortensen's said something to upset you.'

'If that was my reason for leaving, I'd have walked out the day I arrived!'

'Does Mr Harper know you're going?'

'Not yet. He's next on my list.' Not giving herself time to chicken out, she almost ran to the computer-room.

Patrick was in earnest conversation with the Donaldsons, and, beyond a curt nod in her direction, ignored her, his attitude showing he still thought she had wheedled her Rolex out of a foolish old man.

So what? His opinion of her no longer mattered. Patiently she stood her ground, and he finally came across to her.

'Are you waiting for me?'

'Yes. I have to talk to you.'

'Later. I'm up to my eyes.'

'When later?'

He frowned. 'Come to my study at four.'

Knowing the impossibility of doing any work—she was in too much of a state of tension—Tessa returned to Greentrees and packed her cases.

'What did Mr Harper say?' Mrs Benson enquired, watching her push her lunch back and forth across her plate.

'I haven't spoken to him yet. I'm meeting him later.'

'It wasn't such a good joke after all, was it?'

'No, Mrs B. It wasn't.'

Luckily the woman knew when to be quiet, and, grateful for it, Tessa managed to eat a little lunch before going to her room.

At one minute to four, she rapped on the door of Patrick's study and went in. He was sitting behind his desk—barricading himself from her? she wondered—his face stony, his fingertips together.

'I'm leaving today,' she announced baldly.

'You haven't much alternative, have you?'

'Not after the way you're so ready to judge me. You know, Patrick, there's one thing you haven't taken into account. If I were really the gold-digger you think me, I'd have helped myself to a few of the things I found in the attics. You'd never have known, and I could have been thousands of pounds richer.'

'That's true,' he granted. 'I thought of that while I was waiting for you just now.'

'And?' she questioned, hoping this had made him reassess his condemnation of her. Not that it would make any difference to her leaving here. With Ingrid as his lover, there was no future with him for herself.

'I don't think you're a thief, Tessa,' he admitted slowly. 'But I believe you use your youth and—and your not inconsiderable charm, to get what you want.'

His reply gave her the impetus she required to wipe the supercilious smile off his face. When she told him who she was, he would be laughing the other side of it! What pleasure to watch him squirm. Then she would laugh and confess that her entire performance—including her crush on him—had been an act.

'I'm not running away with my tail between my legs,' she began.

'I didn't expect you to. You're nothing if not brazen.'

'And you're a rotten judge of character!'

'If you came in here to have a slanging match, I suggest you go.'

'I intend to. But before I do, I want to tell you you're completely wrong about Mr Anderson and myself.'

'I'm not interested.'

'I think you will be.' Her mouth curved in a smile that only she was aware was false. 'As a matter of fact, I'm Mr Anderson's——'

'Patrick!' The door was flung open and Mike tore into the room, face ashen, eyes wild. 'Come quick! Ingrid fell downstairs. I think she's dying!'

CHAPTER FIFTEEN

FLINGING back his chair, Patrick rushed from the room and down the corridor, Tessa hard on his heels.

Entering the main house, she saw Ingrid crumpled on the floor at the foot of the wide, sweeping staircase. She was unconscious, her right leg twisted awkwardly beneath her, the left one bleeding so heavily that it was a mass of scarlet from the knee down. Her arms were outflung and pieces of shattered glass glittered around her, from a vase she had knocked off a table at the foot of the stairs. Some had penetrated the bodice of her dress and blood was seeping through it.

Patrick bent over her, his skin taking on a greenish tinge. 'I think—I think she's dead!'

Pushing him aside, Tessa felt for the girl's pulse. It was thready and erratic. 'No, she isn't, she's alive. But we have to get her to a hospital at once. Has anyone called an ambulance?'

'I have.' It was Jenna, her voice shaking. 'They said it might take half an hour.'

'Like hell!' Tessa exploded. 'I'll call them myself.'

'I'll do it.' Patrick rose and strode to the phone that stood on a console-table near a suit of armour.

Tessa bent closer over Ingrid and gently unbuttoned the bodice to see the extent of the damage. A long shard of glass had penetrated the chest, causing a narrow but deep wound. Blood was oozing from it, and carefully Tessa eased out the glass.

Her heart was thumping in her throat. This was the stuff of which nightmares were made!

'Ingrid's bleeding fast!' she called across to Patrick. 'Tell them it's urgent!'

As she spoke, she motioned Mike to take off his shirt. Hastily he complied, and she folded it into a pad and pressed it hard against the seeping wound.

'Hold it there for me,' she ordered, taking Mike's hand and placing it in the best position to staunch the red flow.

'Anything *I* can do?' Jenna asked.

'Is there a first-aid box?'

'I'll get it.'

'I'd also like some wide sticks to make a splint,' Tessa called, and Tom Donaldson rushed after his wife.

In less than a minute, they were both back, and Tessa pulled out the widest bandage and methodically applied a tourniquet to Ingrid's leg. The girl moaned, but didn't regain consciousness, which was a good thing for she would have been in considerable pain.

'Keep pressing that chest wound as hard as you can,' Tessa reminded Mike, disturbed that the cotton pad was soaked brilliant red.

'I can't press any harder.' Mike was pale round the mouth. 'Do you think she'll make it?'

Tessa wasn't sure, but deemed it wiser not to say so. Her hands deftly moulded a pile of lint into another pad, and she removed the one Mike was holding and replaced it with the fresh one.

'Keep pressing,' she repeated, rising and going to Patrick, who was still hanging on to the telephone.

'When will the ambulance be here?'

'In half an hour, they think. They're all out on call, and they're trying to locate one.'

'We'll have to take her by car.'

As Patrick went to speak into the receiver, Tessa reached for it.

'There's no need for us both to talk,' he said. 'I'm quite capable of——'

Wrenching the receiver from him, she shouted into it. 'Put me through to the surgical ward. *Don't argue.* Do as I say!'

She paused, waiting to be obeyed, vaguely conscious of the astonishment on the faces around her. The telephone returned to life, a loud, firm voice saying an ambulance would be with them as soon as one was available.

'We can't wait.' Tessa's voice was equally firm. 'My patient has to be operated on immediately. I'm bringing her in myself. If there's no surgeon available when we arrive, *I'll* operate. Of course I'm qualified. Check with St Andrew's Hospital. I'm Tessa Redfern, Sir Denis Denzil's registrar.'

Cutting short the profuse apologies coming from the other end, Tessa put down the receiver.

'We can take Ingrid in the station-wagon,' Patrick said in a voice she hadn't heard before.

She met his eyes briefly, long enough to register their incredulity, but not long enough to decipher more, for she turned away to take the bundle of wide rulers Tom had brought in.

'I'll make a splint for Ingrid's leg,' she said, busy doing so, 'but will someone take down a door for me? We'll use it as a stretcher.'

Ten minutes later they were on their way to Iverton, Patrick's foot hard on the accelerator, Mike's hand hard on the profusely bleeding wound, and Tessa doing her best to staunch the blood seeping from Ingrid's mangled leg.

Her misgivings about the hospital, which was tiny compared with St Andrew's, disappeared at the manner in which their arrival was dealt with. With minimum fuss, Ingrid was placed on a trolley and wheeled to the emergency-room, where a registrar examined her while an X-ray machine was rolled in.

While pictures were taken, and a blood transfusion was being arranged, the surgeon arrived. He had spoken to Sir Denis and was more than happy for Tessa to assist with the operation. She was glad, but hid it. Ingrid's condition had deteriorated, and the gaping wound in her chest and her broken limb had to be attended to speedily if she weren't to bleed to death.

Tessa doubted whether the surgeon—able though he was—had sufficient experience to work at the speed required. Without conceit she knew *she* had, and to the man's credit he recognised it and handed over to her in the operating theatre.

It was dusk by the time they emerged, and not until she had doffed her operating gown did Tessa become conscious of the outer world, and her deep fatigue. She was always like this after a long session in the theatre, but today, having seen Patrick's grey-faced anguish as he watched Ingrid being wheeled away from him, she was more than ever aware of tiredness, and an enervating depression at what she had lost. If one could ever lose what one had never had!

Patrick was pacing the corridor as she came down it. His hair was mussed, his tie awry, but he had never looked handsomer, and it was all she could do not to throw herself into his arms and rest against his chest.

'How is she?' he demanded.

'She'll be fine. She's still unconscious, and being monitored, but you may see her if you wish.'

At his nod, she led him to the intensive care unit, but did not go in with him. It was more than she could bear to watch him beside Ingrid, holding her hand, stroking her skin, caressing her with his eyes.

Numbly, she waited in the corridor, her manner composed and giving away nothing of her feelings as Patrick came out. He appeared more at ease, and there was a little colour in his face.

'Mike, Jenna and Tom wanted to wait, but I sent them home,' he said as they walked towards the exit.

'That was wise.'

'You look as if you can do with a drink,' he went on. 'You were on your feet three hours, at least.'

'That's nothing. I've often done five hours at a stretch. But one rarely feels tired at the time. It isn't until afterwards that it hits you.'

'I can believe it.' He hesitated. 'Would you care to have dinner out and unwind?'

'If I unwind, I'll end up falling asleep at the table! I'd prefer to go straight home, if you don't mind.'

He did not speak again until they were in the station-wagon.

'I think you owe me an explanation, Tessa,' he said gruffly, as they left the hospital car park.

'I know. When I told you this morning that I wanted to speak to you, I was going to confess.'

'What made you put on the act in the first place?'

'Boredom. I had to stop work for three months and elected to stay at my godfather's.'

'Your godfather being Mr Anderson?'

She nodded. 'I was examining the broken wall on your side of the garden when you came along and took it for granted I'd come in answer to your advert. I was amused at the assumptions you made about me, and decided to go along with it. It seemed a fun way of passing the time.'

'A *very* fun way,' he grunted. 'I'm beginning to remember some of the things I said to you.'

'"Butter-fingers" really cut me to the quick!' she made herself laugh. 'And I didn't much care for your casting aspersions on my ability to use a knife!'

'You deserved it, the way you led me up the garden path!'

'I hope you've forgiven me?'

'If you've forgiven *me*.'

'Of course. And, for the record, I'm twenty-seven, not eighteen.'

'You'd make a great fiction writer.'

The ease with which he accepted her explanation and made no reference to the passion they had shared re-awakened her pain. Limbo hadn't lasted long, she thought wryly, and knew it was going to be a long while before she could think of her stay in the country without heartache.

'How much longer will you be on holiday?' Patrick asked. 'I won't suggest you continue being our general dogsbody!'

'I should think not! That's another reason I wanted to speak to you before: to tell you I'm returning to London. I'm fit as a flea and will feel guilty if I take any longer off.'

'A dedicated professional, first and foremost,' he commented.

Her eyes flew to his, but there was no sarcasm in them. 'My work means a lot to me,' she said, grateful he didn't know that behind her calm façade she was weeping for the might-have-beens, the husband she would never have, the children she would never succour.

In silence they drove a few miles, and she tried not to think that after tonight she wasn't likely to see him again, would never hear his voice, never breathe in the smell of him.

'Ingrid owes you her life,' he said suddenly.

'That's overly dramatic. Any surgeon could have done what I did.'

'Not according to Mr Morgan. He was in the intensive unit and I had a word with him. He praised you to the skies.'

'Professional etiquette,' she said hurriedly.

'Why so modest?' Patrick asked. 'The Tessa *I* knew would have been far less so.'

'But you didn't know the real Tessa,' she flashed.

'Too true.'

Nor did I know the real Patrick, she thought bitterly, and was glad when the car stopped outside Greentrees.

'Perhaps you'd make my goodbyes to everyone at the Hall,' she ventured.

'If that's what you wish. But I know they'd like the chance of endorsing *my* thanks for what you did today. I do hope you'll have dinner with us tomorrow night?'

'I'm afraid I can't. I'm leaving for London first thing tomorrow, and I want an early night.' She stepped from the car.

'You don't delay once you make up your mind.' Patrick came to stand beside her.

'Neither do you, I imagine.' She unlocked the front door. 'We both put our work first.'

'At least I also find time to play!' he teased. 'Though, come to think of it, *you* weren't averse to playing a bit either!'

Tessa's breath caught in her throat. At last he had referred to their lovemaking, though from his drawling tone she wished he hadn't.

'How ungallant of you to remind me, Patrick. But you kept talking to me like Methuselah, and I decided to call your bluff.'

'Seems as if we were both having a bit of fun,' he chuckled.

Had she wanted final confirmation of his feelings, she had it now, and it was an effort to keep a tremor from her voice as she spoke.

'I'm so pleased you're taking the hoax in such good part.'

'I can't do otherwise. In your place I might have done the same.'

'You'd make a very bad Man Friday!' She pushed open the front door and moved away from him. 'Don't overwork, though. In the end it can be non-productive.'

'Yes, Doctor.' His laugh drifted behind him as he returned to the station-wagon. 'I hope you won't forget to listen to your own advice.'

'I won't,' she promised, and made herself stay where she was until the tail-lights disappeared into the darkness.

Only then did she enter the house and close the door, leaning against it as if it could give her strength.

'My love,' she whispered. 'My lost love.'

CHAPTER SIXTEEN

'TESSA, what a surprise! You look marvellous!' was Sir Denis's instant comment when he entered his consulting-rooms at the hospital and saw Tessa talking to his secretary. 'In town for the day?' he enquired, leading her into his room.

'In town permanently.' She was delighted her appearance didn't pity her. 'I'm fighting fit and ready to start work.'

Lips pursed, he surveyed her, and, as if satisfied with what he saw, nodded agreement. 'I hope there's a young man in the offing?'

'Afraid not. I just relaxed and read and ate.'

'Ah, well, as long you don't slip back into your old routine and take on too much.'

'You're a fine one to talk,' she chided. 'Your workload is worse than mine.'

'But when I switch off, I do so completely. *You're* inclined to come in and find extra work.'

'Not any more, I won't,' she assured him. 'I've learned my lesson.'

Despite this avowal, Tessa slipped into the frenetic hospital routine as though she had never left it and, once back into the swing of things, found it impossible to switch off, a fact which Sir Denis noted without comment.

To be honest she made little effort, considering work her best means of forgetting Patrick.

Fat chance of that, she conceded at the end of the month, for he came to the forefront of her mind the instant she left the hospital each evening, and only faded from it when she returned there each morning.

She knew she should make an effort to build a private life, but, since it was impossible to imagine herself with any man other than Patrick, it seemed a pointless exercise. The years stretched before her, with nothing to show for them other than professional accolades and personal aridity.

Would their story have ended the same way if she had not had a career, or been willing to give it up for marriage? But that was presupposing Patrick's relationship with Ingrid was over. Yet, even if it were, the question was worthless, for her work was an integral part of her life, and she could no more abandon it than stop breathing.

Their only hope of a future together would have been for Patrick to have made the adjustment—not easy, bearing in mind his much-vaunted objection to working wives.

In reality her career would have created little problem for either of them. He put in long hours of concentrated effort, and she could as easily have spent that time in hospital as whiling it away in his house, where his staff ran everything with clockwork precision.

Yet such thoughts were pie in the sky. There was no chance of his changing his thinking, because he didn't love her. If he did, he would have found a reason to contact her.

Gradually, as the weeks turned into months, there were entire days when she didn't think of him. At this rate, she'd forget him completely within a few years!

In the middle of October, Mrs Benson telephoned to say Henry was going into the veterinary hospital in London to have an operation on his hip.

'I took him there this morning, and they will be operating on him tomorrow.'

'Poor Henry. Do they think he'll make a complete recovery?'

'He'll be as good as new, they said. But they'll be keeping him there for two weeks, and I was hoping you——'

'Don't worry, Mrs B., I'll visit him twice a week.'

'You're a good girl, Tessa. I'll come to see him too, and if we fit in with each other he'll see a face he knows nearly every day.'

Talking to Mrs Benson made Tessa realise how much she missed Greentrees and her godfather. He was still in New Zealand and proposed spending the worst part of the British winter there.

'Why not fly out and join me for Christmas?' he had suggested, and, though she hadn't agreed to go, she was toying with the idea.

It was out of the question for her to go to Greentrees. She might not necessarily bump into Patrick, but simply being near his home would be unbearable. She'd have to come to terms with this when Uncle Martin returned in March, but as of now her emotional stability was too fragile for her to put further strain on it.

In her efforts to stop thinking of him, she sought out old friends from medical school. The only trouble with this was that many of them were married and did their best to pair her off with the unattached men they knew. Unfortunately she automatically compared each one with Patrick—finding him infinitely handsomer and more intelligent. None the less, she compelled herself to accept every reasonable invitation proffered her. After all, it was childish to assume only one man was suitable for her!

She had almost convinced herself she was totally re-covered when she picked up an evening paper and saw Patrick's face smiling out of it. It appeared his company had won an export award, and there was talk of his re-ceiving a knighthood. Ingrid was going to cling to him like a limpet—if they weren't already married!

Tessa scanned the article, but found no mention of a wife—no mention of anything personal, in fact, for it concentrated on his brilliant technological achievements.

Scrunching the paper, she threw it into the waste-paper basket, but an hour later she retrieved it and did her best to straighten it out, staring hungrily into the fine-boned face, with its thin but shapely mouth, long, firm nose and deep-set eyes. Despite this flashbulb shot, his charm was tangible, and a wave of such desolation washed over her that she was swamped by it.

The following day she was glad to find she had a heavier than usual operating schedule, for it left her no opportunity for moping, and it was well past eight o'clock when she returned to her consulting-room, hungry and exhausted, and sank into an easy chair.

Kicking off her pumps, she wriggled her toes, sighing with pleasure as she did. Then she reached for the thermos of coffee left for her by her secretary, and poured herself a cup. A plate of smoked salmon sand-wiches, cling-wrapped and inviting, awaited her too, but for the moment she was too tired to eat. Instead she sipped the hot coffee and mulled over the day.

A soft knock on the door brought her out of her reverie, and she frowned. If there was an emergency with one of her patients, she would be bleeped, so it was probably one of the housemen anxious to further his knowledge by picking her brains.

Slipping into her shoes, she called for him to come in.

The tall, slender woman who did brought Tessa jumping to her feet.

'Miss Mortensen!' She didn't know what else to say, and stared at Ingrid dumbly. Then common sense took over, and she spoke again. 'I'm glad you've fully recovered. Mr Morgan, your surgeon, kept me informed about your progress.'

'Yes, he told me. He also said you did a brilliant job on my chest and leg.'

Tessa made a disclaiming gesture. The warm smile on Ingrid's face, in place of the familiar enmity, was proof the girl was no longer jealous of her, which meant she must be completely sure of Patrick. The desolation that swamped Tessa at this was proof positive she had nowhere near stopped loving him. So much for her belief that she had!

'I'm sorry I didn't telephone before coming,' Ingrid was saying, 'but I wasn't sure if you'd agree to see me.'

Tessa made herself laugh. 'You were a tough lady to work for, but I don't blame you for it. I guess I was quite a trial to you!'

Ingrid laughed too, and sat down, crossing one leg over the other and smoothing her skirt. She was as beautiful as ever, her hair—worn in a softer, curlier style—made her look younger than the twenty-six she was, and her skin gleamed with the lustre of a pearl.

I can't hold a candle to her, Tessa granted morosely, and wished she knew exactly what had melted the Swedish girl's coldness.

'I was amazed when Patrick told me your true identity,' Ingrid said into the silence. 'You must have thoroughly enjoyed making fools of us.'

'It *was* rather amusing.' Tessa wished there were some folders in front of her, enabling her to plead pressure of work and end this meeting. But she was stuck, and had to make the best of it. 'Would you care for a coffee?'

'No, thanks, I'm awash with it. I was waiting in Reception for two hours. It didn't enter my head you'd be working this late.'

'I frequently work far later.'

'I see.' The pale eyes flickered. 'I was hoping to come and talk to you weeks ago, to thank you for saving my life, but I was up to my eyes with work.'

'There's no need to apologise. You wrote and thanked me, which was quite enough.'

'Nothing's enough for what you did. You saved my life, and I wanted to thank you face to face.'

'I was only doing my job.'

'There's no "only" about it. Fate must have brought you to work at the Hall. If you hadn't been there I'd have bled to death!'

'I doubt it,' Tessa demurred.

'I don't. You saved my life.'

'I hope you didn't come to London especially to say this?' Tessa said jocularly.

'I did. Otherwise I would have gone directly to Heathrow Airport.'

'You're going abroad?' The question slipped out and Tessa was mortified with herself, though Ingrid didn't appear to notice.

'I'm going to Sweden to say goodbye to my family. I'm off to Australia for the next three years.'

Tessa's heart thumped painfully. 'Is Patrick moving there, then?'

'No.' Ingrid's pale eyes studied the floor. 'You've got it wrong. You see, I'm leaving him.'

'Leaving? But why? I——' Tessa caught herself up. 'Forgive me, it's none of my business.'

'Actually, it is.'

Tessa was startled, but managed to hide it, afraid of giving vent to curiosity in case she gave away her feelings.

'It's *you* he cares for,' Ingrid said flatly.

'I beg your pardon?'

'Patrick. He loves you.'

'I can't believe that.'

'I don't blame you, after the way I behaved.'

Careful to mask her expression, Tessa met Ingrid's eyes. 'I'm afraid I don't follow you.'

'You will when you've heard me out. You see, you misjudged that scene you saw through the window of Patrick's sitting-room.'

Tessa swallowed hard. Should she play ignorant and deny witnessing it? She was debating the point when Ingrid spoke again.

'I'd gone to talk to Patrick that night and saw you coming across the lawn. I was pretty certain you'd pass the window, and I shammed a faint and collapsed on the settee. Patrick bent over me and I pulled him into my arms. Short of hurting me, he couldn't break free, and by the time he did you'd gone.'

'It struck me as a very passionate embrace,' Tessa remarked.

'On my side only. If you saw me clinging hard, it's because he was trying equally hard to throw me off!'

'Why did you do it?'

'Do you honestly need to ask?' Ingrid said drily. 'I was determined to make sure *you* didn't get him. It was obvious he was attracted to you, and, though I knew he thought you too young and irresponsible, I was still worried he'd fall for you. I've loved him for years, and he was beginning to see me as a woman, not merely his assistant, when *you* turned up. I was desperate to get you out of the way, and I didn't care how I did it. It wasn't until after my accident, when I realised I owed my life to you...' Ingrid leaned forward, her expression earnest. 'But I still couldn't bring myself to tell you the truth because I hadn't given up hope.'

'Then why are you here now?'

'I finally accepted he wasn't interested in me as a woman.'

Tessa was uncertain what to say. Her earlier dislike of Ingrid, though tempered today, none the less made it difficult for her to disclose her feelings. Yet she had to say something, and chose the least innocuous comment.

'So Patrick was attracted to me,' she shrugged. 'That doesn't mean much.'

'More than attraction. I've just told you. I saw how he looked at you when you weren't aware of it. I don't expect you to confide in me, Tessa, but if you do care for him, tell him.'

'Does he know you were coming here?'

'No.'

Tessa stared down at her hands. 'The—er—the feelings you say he has for me, did he—has he discussed them with you?'

'Patrick isn't the type to talk to one woman about another. But I know him well enough to be sure how he feels.'

'Do you?' Tessa asked drily. 'Until a few weeks ago you believed you had a chance with him.'

'I was fooling myself. Then one morning I faced the truth and knew it was time for me to make a fresh start.' Ingrid rose. 'I've said my piece. What you do with it is your affair. But if you do have any feelings for Patrick, don't let pride stand in your way.'

Without another word, she walked out, and Tessa leaned back in her chair and sighed. If it were only her pride that was involved, she would go to him this very

minute and open her heart. But there was her work—
which meant a great deal to her—and there was Patrick's
deeply rooted objection to a wife with a career.

It was a barrier she could see no way around.

CHAPTER SEVENTEEN

KNOWING Patrick hadn't been making love to Ingrid that night certainly lessened Tessa's anger towards him, but she remained reluctant to do anything about it.

If he loved her, as Ingrid said, confessing *she* loved *him* wasn't going to dissolve the basic problem between them: his adamant abhorrence of having a working wife.

Yet even this was jumping the gun, for last time they had spoken intimately he had made it clear he valued his freedom too much to tie himself down in the foreseeable future.

Regardless of how often she reminded herself of this, Tessa found it impossible to dismiss what Ingrid had said. She pictured him alone at the Hall and ached to be with him, to have him hold her, touch her.

Who cared if he insisted on remaining single? She wanted him so badly that she was prepared to settle for living with him. Except living with him as his girlfriend was likely to present as many difficulties as living with him as his wife, for she would insist on continuing her career, and he would fret and fume if she wasn't available whenever he wanted her. Damn his obstinacy!

For the next week Tessa wrestled with herself, one moment on the verge of dropping everything and haring off to see Patrick, the next dismissing the issues that divided them as unresolvable.

'You're looking frazzled again,' Sir Denis commented on the Thursday, studying her pale face and too-slender frame. 'Haven't you learned your lesson not to overwork?'

'I'm not doing more than you,' she protested.

'Maybe. But you're doing it with unnecessary intensity.' His eyes narrowed with curiosity. 'You haven't fallen in love, have you?'

Momentarily she hesitated, then nodded. 'I regret to say I have, and it's killing me!'

'Why? Is he married?'

'Oh, no.'

Sir Denis waited, not pressing her, and Tessa, aware that his interest was well meant, debated whether to confide in him. Disclosing her innermost feelings to him didn't come easily to her, for she always kept her emotional life apart from her professional one. Yet with her godfather away—he was her greatest mentor and confidant—she needed to confide in someone she trusted, and whose opinion she valued.

Haltingly, she told him of her charade, alive to the amusement on his face as she did, though his smile disappeared as her story continued.

'So you see,' she concluded, 'it's hopeless. If Patrick and I just lived together, he'd still expect me to devote myself to him. He recently bought into a company in the States, and will probably be spending a fair amount of time there, which means he'd expect me to go with him.'

'Has he said so?'

'No, but——'

'Then why anticipate it?'

'Because I know how he thinks. He said it often enough.'

'Was he in love with you when he expounded his opinions?'

'I'm not certain. He was always attracted to me, but I don't honestly know when it became love. Because he thought I was a teenager, he was fighting it.'

'You don't say!' Sir Denis chuckled. 'Pity I didn't see you in your miniskirt or baggy pants! I bet you were very fetching.'

'Not fetching enough to bring him to the boil,' came Tessa's dry comment.

'Don't be too sure,' her chief argued. 'By all accounts he was bubbling along nicely! If you hadn't misunderstood the scene you witnessed through the window, you might well have brought him to boiling-point. It was unfortunate that the moment the poor man discovered your true identity you upped and left without giving him a chance to reassess his feelings for you.'

'I only left because I was fooled by the stunt Ingrid pulled. But, regardless of that, Patrick has had months to think things over, and if he cared for me in the slightest he wouldn't have given up on me. He's a fighter,' she added by way of explanation.

'Perhaps he is also a realist. You can be very persuasive when you set yourself to it, Tessa, and you probably convinced him you don't care for him in the slightest.'

'If he loved me enough he'd at least make an effort to win me.'

'If *you* loved *him* enough, you'd make an effort too.'

'It's not the same thing.'

'Indeed?' Sir Denis raised an eyebrow. 'From where I stand, you and this Patrick of yours have similar problems to overcome. He doesn't believe you love him, and you don't believe Ingrid when she says he does!'

Tessa shook her head, her soft, red-gold curls in disarray. 'You're muddling me!'

'You are muddling yourself. Be logical, my dear. You tell me that if he loved you he'd fight for you. *Ergo*, if you love him, you will do the same!'

'It's more than a question of love,' Tessa sighed. 'My profession is the stumbling block. He won't accept it.'

Sir Denis put a hand on her shoulder. 'What a man says when he fancies a girl is often quite different from what he says when he faces the fact that he loves her. In my salad days I set my heart on marrying a blonde, like my mother. I refused to take out a girl unless she was at least mousy! Yet whom did I marry?'

Tessa gave a wry smile; Lady Denzil hailed from Rio, and her hair was black as night!

'Think over what I've said,' he concluded. 'And remember, faint heart never won obstinate tycoon!'

That evening, Tessa mulled over her conversation with Sir Denis. Frequently her hand hovered over the telephone, but she couldn't quite find the courage to call Patrick. She switched on the news, and was trying to concentrate on it when Mrs Benson called to say Henry was well enough to leave the hospital, and she was collecting him the following day.

'Unless, of course, you plan on coming here for the weekend and will bring him with you,' the woman said wistfully. 'It's lonely here without Mr Anderson.'

Guilt prodded Tessa's conscience, and on the spur of the moment she agreed to collect the dog and bring him down.

'I'm operating till five,' she finished, 'so don't expect us till eight at the earliest.'

The instant a happy Mrs Benson rang off, Tessa bitterly regretted her offer. Until she definitely decided what to do about Patrick, it was crazy to go to Greentrees. But it was too late to back out of it now.

First thing next morning she asked her secretary to inform the veterinary hospital she would collect Henry later that evening. Unfortunately an emergency delayed her, and it was nearly ten before she returned to her apartment with him—too late to drive to the country.

Excitedly Henry pushed past her into the hallway, tail wagging as he bounded over the weekend case Mrs Harris, her housekeeper, had packed ready for her.

Holding his collar tightly, Tessa tried to pull him away from the sitting-room door, which he was avidly sniffing. But he was big and she was tired, and it wasn't until she remembered to utter the magic word 'dinner' that he allowed himself to be led into the kitchen.

Leaving him happily munching through a bowl of mince and cereal, Tessa called Mrs Benson to say she wasn't leaving till next morning, then made herself an omelette.

While she ate, she came to the conclusion that destiny was taking her to Greentrees, and it was foolish not to take advantage of it and at least pop in on Patrick. Any further move was dependent on his reaction to her. If he appeared pleased by her visit, she would be frank with him about her feelings; if he acted cool, she would be cooler.

Leaving Henry snoozing on an old blanket, she cleared away the dishes, then decided to go into the sitting-room to watch the late night news.

Opening the door, she stopped dead.

Patrick lay fast asleep on the sofa! From the empty coffee-cup on the floor beside him, she guessed her daily housekeeper had let him in before she left, and he had literally got tired of waiting for her!

She moved over to waken him, then drew back and stared into his face. He was paler and thinner than she remembered, and his grey tweed trousers and light grey sweater suggested he had not come to London for a business meeting, but was here only to see her.

Bending lower, she feasted her eyes on him, then felt guilty for studying him while he slept. But it was an opportunity not to be missed, and her eyes lingered lovingly on the lock of chestnut hair fallen on his forehead, the long lashes splayed fanlike on the hollow cheeks, the straight, classic nose, the upturned, humorous mouth. It was his smile that always affected her more than anything else. And those blue eyes. She longed for him to open them, but not yet. She was going to savour this moment as long as possible.

Quietly she sat in the armchair opposite him. But not as quietly as she thought, for he shifted, gave a grunt and sat up, instantly wide awake.

'Tessa!' Impatiently he raked back the hair from his forehead. 'Sorry, I must have fallen asleep.'

'Not to worry.' She was carefully casual, wary at finding him in her apartment. She longed to ask why he was here, but resolutely refused to do so.

'I must be more tired than I thought,' he went on, sounding irritated with himself. 'But when your housekeeper informed me you were going away for the weekend, I was scared of missing you and waited.'

'Care for a sandwich or another coffee?'

'I've already had both.'

'I'm not counting!'

'The hell with food! That isn't why I'm here.'

He jumped to his feet and paced the floor with nervous movements. He was so obviously ill at ease and unlike the sophisticated man she knew that she waited on tenterhooks.

'You're looking great,' he said abruptly. 'Blooming, in fact.'

So much for his perception! However, she nodded her thanks at the compliment.

'You're looking fine too,' she replied, playing him at his own game.

'I don't feel it. I can't sleep, I can't concentrate, I can't do any damn thing except——' He stopped, then said at a tangent, 'I was hoping you'd come to your godfather's house one weekend.'

'It's rather pointless when he isn't there. I only went before because I was convalescing.'

'Instead of which you worked your butt off at the Hall!'

'Hardly work, Patrick. A vacation compared with what I do at St Andrews!'

'Ah, I was forgetting the hospital.' He cleared his throat on the word, frowning fiercely. 'It's very important to you, isn't it?'

'Yes.' She was finding it increasingly difficult to hide her feelings for him, and, visualising this conversation going nowhere for the next hour, took the plunge. 'Why have you come here, Patrick? What are you trying to tell me?'

'That I love you and can't live without you.'

There was dead silence. Their eyes met, but neither of them moved. He because he was waiting for her reaction; she because she was waiting for him to elaborate.

'I'm aware the—er—the whole thing was a charade for you,' he went on jerkily, his hand pulling at his shirt-collar as though it were choking him. 'But for me it was... What I mean is, I didn't realise what was happening to me until I—er——' He cleared his throat and began again. 'I made myself fight my feelings for you because I believed you were only eighteen, but I wasn't too successful, as you know.' He paused, as if waiting for her to speak, and when she didn't, exploded, 'Dammit, Tessa! Don't you know what I'm trying to tell you? Didn't my kisses make it plain?'

She almost flung herself into his arms, only restrained by the fear that he still expected her to fall in with his image of an ideal wife.

'You once warned me not to read too much into your kisses,' she reminded him.

'I was lying! A desperate attempt to fool you—and myself as well.' He took a step towards her. 'How can you sit there so calmly? At least show surprise, if nothing else! Or did you already guess how I feel?'

'I'm not clairvoyant.' Tessa rose. It brought her close to him, emphasising the difference in their height, and forcing her to tilt her head to watch his face. 'After Ingrid's accident, when you discovered my identity and we said goodbye, why didn't you give me an inkling that you cared for me?'

'Pride,' he stated baldly. 'You acted as if you couldn't wait to get away.'

'What's happened to your pride now?'

'I bet you enjoy probing with a scalpel,' he muttered, turning away from her. 'Go on, laugh at me. I deserve it.'

The pain in his voice was too much for her, and with an incoherent murmur she bridged the short distance between them and clasped her arms around his waist.

'I love you,' she said into his rigid back. 'I have almost from the moment I met you.'

With an exclamation he swung round. 'Then it wasn't all an act, as you said?'

'No. But I had pride too.'

He groaned and pulled her close. 'What a lot of time we've wasted.' His body was trembling, his skin damp from emotion as he spoke. 'Tessa, Tessa, these past months have been hell for me.'

'For me too.'

She lifted her face and his head lowered to hers. Their lips met, their touch tentative, as if neither was sure of the other. But as their mouths remained close and his breath mingled with hers, the urgency of their desire for each other surfaced. Their hands moved to touch, legs to twine, bodies to merge, and suddenly they were devouring each other with long, drugging kisses as tongues explored and sweet moisture was absorbed.

With a groan, Patrick pushed her away, though he kept his hands on her. 'Darling, we have to talk.'

Fear drew the blood from her head and she went dizzy. The moment she had dreaded was here, and, aware she couldn't continue running away from it, she allowed him to draw her on to the settee beside him. He did not speak, and her fear deepened as she waited.

Scanning her set face, he expelled his breath on a sigh. 'I don't have to say it, do I?'

'No.' Her voice was faint and she cleared her throat and said it again. 'No, you don't.'

'Good.' His relief was palpable. 'All we have to decide on now is a date for the wedding. As far as I'm concerned, the quieter the better.'

'No, Patrick!' Pulling her hand free of his, she jumped to her feet. 'I can't agree to it.'

'Then I'll leave it to you, darling. But it means us facing a barrage of publicity and——'

'I'm not talking of our marriage!' she cried. 'There won't be one anyway.'

'Tessa!' He reached for her, but she evaded him.

'It won't work, Patrick. Even if I agree to do as you ask, I'll never manage to stick to it. I love you with all my heart, but I can't turn my back on the gift I was born with.' Helplessly she began to cry, uncaring that he saw, feeling she was being torn in two and would never be whole again.

'Darling, don't!' He was beside her, his voice pleading as he put his arms around her.

She yearned to lean against him, but instead tried to pull away, scared lest the touch of his body should weaken her resolve and make her utter worthless promises.

Aware of her resistance, he tightened his hold. 'You've got it wrong, my love. I'm not expecting you to stop being a surgeon. Did you think that's what I meant?'

'Yes.' Slowly she raised her head. 'You always said you didn't want a wife with a career.'

'Shows what a bigoted fool I was!' Taking a handkerchief from his pocket, he wiped away her tears. 'I've changed my opinions, Tessa.'

'Because you have to.' Her sadness was in her voice, and, hearing it, he gave her a little shake.

'That's not true. If I felt as I did months ago, I'd probably try to lay down the law again. But I *have* changed. When you walked out of my life, when I believed I meant nothing to you, I touched rock-bottom.' He paused, his eyes darkening with the memory of it. 'I went through hell. Tough enough and hot enough to burn away my stupid prejudices. I don't fancy a bimbo as a wife. I need a woman who can match me mentally as well as satisfy me physically. Who is a person in her own right. And if she considers it her right to be a doctor, a baker, or a candlestick maker, then I'll happily accept it and will do whatever I have to to make the marriage work.'

Listening to this impassioned statement, Tessa didn't doubt he meant what he said. But would he feel the same when they were man and wife and the first flush of passion was over?

As if privy to her thoughts, he dropped his arms away from her and went to stand by the bookshelf. 'I'm not

saying all this in the heat of desire. I've thought it out
from every angle, I promise you. I'm not saying it's going
to be easy, Tessa. There will be many occasions when
I'll resent your work, be irritated because you can't come
with me on my travels. But as compensation I'll have a
wife who is a happy and satisfied woman—which will
be worth whatever compromises I have to make.'

Only then did Tessa's fear die. Hearing Patrick weigh
up the pros had worried her; hearing him admit the cons
reassured her totally.

'I'm prepared to compromise too,' she said, moving
towards him. 'Marriage is a partnership, Patrick, and I
intend playing *my* part in it. I'll lessen my workload,
and when you go on long trips I *will* go with you.'

'You won't find me giving you an argument on that!'

'We'll never argue.'

'Yes, we will. But the making up will be wonderful!'
He hugged her tightly. 'Thank God the career question
is settled. Now let's change the subject.'

'Did you ever go to bed with Ingrid?'

'What?'

'You said we should change the subject!'

'Not to that. She's in the past.'

'You haven't answered my question though.'

'Will you believe me if I say I haven't?'

'Yes.'

'Good. And the answer is no, I never have. I suppose
I was tempted at the very beginning when she first came
to work for me, but it's my policy not to mix business
with pleasure.' He grinned. 'Though I did it with you,
come to think of it. But then you were special.'

'I was?'

'Let me show you *how* special,' he said ardently,
rubbing his thighs upon hers.

'That's just what the doctor was going to order!'

They didn't make it to the bedroom. Passion flared fast and strong, overwhelming them and flinging them into a vortex which spun them out of control. His broken apologies were negated by her passionate urging as she matched him movement for movement, her body expanding to accept him, her smallness tight around him, sheathing him, inflaming him until he was no longer in control and exploded within her in a gush of fire that pervaded every fibre of her being.

They came to their senses on the floor, and as she moved gingerly he raised his head from her breast and levered himself off her.

'Did I hurt you?' he questioned huskily. 'You're so small and fragile, I——'

'It was wonderful.' Her eyes were misty. 'I wish I were more experienced for you.'

'I don't.' His mouth found her tumescent nipples, moving from one to the other as he sucked them into hard peaks. 'I never thought I'd be the first,' he admitted.

'Someone had to be!'

'At the risk of being called a chauvinist pig, I have to say I'm glad it was me.'

'So am I.'

She stroked his thick, chestnut hair, then let her fingers glide over the strong back. His body stirred and she felt the powerful surge of his desire, giving a little gasp as, with one swift movement, he rose with her in his arms and strode into her bedroom.

'I can't have you complaining of a bad back!' he murmured into her mouth, and, laying her gently upon the bed, began caressing her.

This time he took her slowly, refusing her urgent pleas to enter her, quieting his movements when she became too aroused, and gradually bringing her to such a trembling peak of desire that she was begging for him as he slowly, slowly penetrated her.

His manhood was as teasing as the tongue stroking the hollow between her breasts, entering and withdrawing until she frenziedly clutched at his buttocks and pulled them hard down, the movement pushing him deeper into her. His shout of ecstasy was her victory, for he was too far gone to withdraw, and swelled and throbbed against the soft cavern of her womb.

'Stay still,' he pleaded thickly, and she did as he asked, remaining motionless until the conquered became the conqueror once again. Only when he grew and thickened did she teasingly gyrate her hips, the fierce contractions of her body leading him to the brink and beyond as, with another great cry, the liquid of his life gushed into her.

Tessa awoke first, enjoying the sight of Patrick's head on the pillow next to her, and the weight of his hand on the softness of her belly. He still looked tired and pale, but his features were relaxed, and there was a calmness in his sleeping face which had not been there previously.

Her tummy rumbled and she became aware of being hungry. The bedside clock showed midnight, and ruefully she remembered her supper of two eggs. Not much sustenance bearing in mind the energy she had just expended! Pretty sure Patrick was also going to be hungry when he awoke, she carefully slid from the bed, donned a housecoat and went into the kitchen.

As she turned on the light, Henry lifted his head and thumped his tail on the floor.

'Good morning to you too,' she said happily. 'But be a good boy and go back to sleep.'

The shaggy head lowered on to the two front paws, and soulful eyes followed her from refrigerator to table to sink. Heart melting, Tessa dropped him a piece of the cold chicken she was slicing for sandwiches, and when a plate was piled high and set on a tray, together with a thermos of hot soup, she carried it into the bedroom.

She didn't get beyond the door. Convulsed with silent laughter, she watched as Henry, lying full length next to Patrick, was busily licking his idol's ear.

'Mmm,' Patrick murmured, his back moving erotically. 'Don't stop, sweetheart.'

Responding to the soft tone, Henry's licking grew more enthusiastic.

'Mmm,' Patrick repeated. 'Where did you learn that little trick?' Eyes still closed, he turned. 'Come closer, sweetheart.'

As he put out a languid arm for her, his fingers clasped a furry body. With a roar he opened his eyes, and with another roar leapt from the bed and took a swipe at Henry.

Limp with laughter, Tessa nearly dropped the tray.

'I'm glad you find it funny,' Patrick bit out, chasing Henry from the room and closing the door. 'What the hell's this damn dog doing here?'

'He had an operation on his hip, and I'm taking him back to Greentrees.'

Patrick stared at her askance. 'Don't tell me you operated on Henry!'

'Don't be ridiculous.' She choked back another gust of laughter.

'I don't wish to see hair nor hide of that hound once we're married!' he asserted. 'If necessary I'll electrify the wall round the house.'

'You wouldn't!'

'Try me.'

'Not till I've drunk my soup. I'm starving.'

'That wasn't what I——' He halted, a smile tugging the corner of his mouth. 'It's a good thing you didn't have a video camera to record this little scene.'

'It would certainly have given our children a good laugh!'

Sandwich raised to his mouth, Patrick stopped. 'Another comment like that, and you won't be eating for another hour!'

'All I mentioned were children!'

He lunged for her and brought her down on the bed. 'That does it!'

His body heavy on hers, she stared into his blue, blue eyes.

'Know something?' she said in a little-girl voice. 'I'm not in the least bit hungry!'

◈ *Harlequin Presents*

is

- ☑ exotic
- ☑ dramatic
- ☑ sensual
- ☑ exciting
- ☑ contemporary
- ☑ a fast, involving read
- ☑ terrific!!

*Harlequin Presents—
passionate romances
around the world!*